ANDREW AND THE ALCHEMIST

ANDREW AND THE ALCHEMIST

By Barbara Ninde Byfield

Illustrated by Deanne Hollinger

Doubleday & Company, Inc.,
Garden City, New York

Library of Congress Cataloging in Publication Data

Byfield, Barbara Ninde.
    Andrew and the alchemist.

    SUMMARY: Andrew, an eleven-year-old orphan,
becomes apprenticed to an alchemist and begins a
life of adventure.
    [1. Alchemists—Fiction.   2. Magic—Fiction]
I. Hollinger, Deanne.   II. Title.
PZ7.B986An   [Fic]
ISBN: 0-385-12233-0 Trade
      0-385-12234-9 Prebound
Library of Congress Catalog Card Number 76-7694

Designed by LAURENCE ALEXANDER

For
Frank Tedeschi

To an Adept
from a Venerable

ANDREW AND THE ALCHEMIST

Chapter I

Andrew lay huddled in more misery than his eleven years had known could exist, hoping against hope that this would be the dawn wolves would finally eat him alive. He was much too cold to wake up and think about it properly, much less say a prayer. If what the townspeople had been saying were true, it was more than likely that the coldest winter in memory would drive the ravenous beasts from their mountain lairs into the town in search of food, particularly homeless orphans.

Andrew was willing to be eaten. The grudging trickle of warm air coming up through the street-level basement window against which he was lying was barely enough to keep him alive, and smelt dreadfully of bad eggs anyway. He had spent the two previous nights sleeping around the corner in the shed of a Mr. Grundage, Undertaker. It held a supply of empty coffins, which provided Andrew with some protection against the bitter cold. But Grundage had discovered him this morning and, like all the townsfolk Andrew had encountered since his arrival, ejected him with panic, fright, and a kick and blow or two to make the point that he was not wanted.

Even the pawnbroker, who had given Andrew a few thin coins for his little brass hand bell, had looked at him with suspicion and shooed him out of the shop as soon as he could. The hand bell was—had been—Andrew's only possession left. His father had, as usual, sent Andrew ahead on the snowy road down into the town to ring the bell, advertising the momentary arrival of Thomas the Tinker, Pots & Pans Mended, Knives Ground, Scissors Sharpened, & All Manner of Metal Work! The jaunty tinker's wagon, laden with anvils, grindstones, tools, and a small stove as well as their clothes and beds, was to have followed shortly after. Old Thumble, the horse, wasn't too fast any more, especially on the icy roads, and Andrew left them just topping the mountain pass. As he scampered on ahead, he stopped for his breath in the high mountain air and looked back. Just in time to hear the gray-green terror of a thunderclap, followed by the slow, awesome, peeling away of snow, ice, and glacier from the top of the mountain, the avalanche falling faster and faster, swallowing up his father, the wagon, and old Thumble in its irrevocable harvest to the valley.

The small coins Andrew had been given for the hand bell had bought only two stale rolls and a half can of thin blue milk, little enough food for a growing lad who had run on into the town, shocked, grieving, frightened and above all, cold to the bone, a new orphan alone in a strange town. And that had been day before yesterday—or longer. It was hard to remember precisely, Andrew thought, when all you could think about was food.

So, after the irate Mr. Grundage had threatened to set his dogs on him, and whacked Andrew with a stick as he clambered out of the coffin, Andrew had run through the hillside town, vaguely aware of a splendid small palace sitting atop a cliff, with the streets of the town spreading down and behind the palace walls like a comfortable lap, but doors were closed tight and many windows shuttered too; there was no place for him.

He was tempted to throw himself into the lake which stretched from the palace's cliff and the town walls to the far side of the valley, but even there, there was no place for him. The lake was frozen solid, black. In his hunger and cold he couldn't be sure, but surely the lake was higher, fuller, than when he and Pappy had topped the pass? He thought he remembered a much smaller lake, almost a pond, with stony, infertile shores and scruffy pastureland full of dead thistles. The mountainsides themselves were covered with farmhouses, barns, silos, and sheepsheds which looked prosperous even under their blankets of snow. What did it matter? he asked himself, shoving away the thought of the terrible avalanche and turning up a narrow, winding street that ended in a high stone wall, with a modest town house shuttered tightly against the gloom. It was here he had espied the street-level window, around the corner from the house's stoop, and snuggled up against it, tired, hungry, and in no mood to wonder why anyone would leave a window—even a cellar window—open in such cold.

Yes, the wolves were finally at him. He was more frozen than asleep, but he felt the first sharp poke of their fangs in the back of his knees, then his backside. Half-consciously he thought, I hope they get it over with soon—then I can see old Pappy and Thumble again. . . .

The Venerable P. C. Delver, Adept, squinted, took off his half-moon spectacles, wiped them on his sleeve, settled them back halfway down his rather large nose, and resumed his task of measuring a sackful of pulverized antimony into drachms, scruples, minims, and modicums.

Dash it all, he thought to himself, hearing the morning Angelus ring faintly, should be lighter than this by now. Can't see a thing. He shuffled over to the crucible of bubbling brimstone under the small window set high in the cellar's wall, propped open slightly to let the odorous fumes out into the bitter winter air.

Delver removed the crucible with a pair of tongs and set it on the floor to cool. So that's why it's so dark, he thought, looking up through the little window at a bundle of rags and sticks lying against the window's grill, shutting off his light. Must have blown there during the night while I was working in the back.

He found a longish poker among a collection hanging on the fireplace wall, and reached up to poke the trash away. Beelzebub, it *was* cold. The morning air flowed down the inside of his sleeve as he pushed the poker up firmly. But it didn't budge the bundle of rags and, sighing, he took a deep breath and gave it a real twist and jab. Not being young—in point of fact being quite, quite old indeed—he did try to conserve his strength, and hoped this time the wind would help the clutter blow away.

Instead, the bundle gathered itself up with a low moan, interrupted by unmistakably chattering teeth. A foot, in a thin boot wrapped partly around with old rags, dangled through the grill and window.

"Who's that up there, eh? Hmm? Move on, can't you? You're in my light. I say, you're in my light. Can't see a thing."

A small, tousled head with straw-matted hair peered down, nose and lips blue with cold. "Oh, oh —I *could* move on, but you see, sir, if I do that I'll freeze to death. It's only your warm air coming up through the window that's kept me alive so far—"

Oh, drat it all—Delver thought crossly, one interruption after another. "You sure you have *no* place else to go? Tried the church?"

"Yessir, but it's stone, you know, and colder inside than out, and they lock it up at night anyway. I was all right until yesterday; I slept in the coffins down the street but Mr. Grundage chased me off. I stuffed my jacket with his wood shavings and sawdust, and my boots with straw, but it doesn't help much."

Something hard and blue dropped at one fur-shod foot of The Venerable P. C. Delver, and shattered. A frozen tear.

Drat and blast. "Well, come down, boy, come down. Around the corner and under the stoop . . . dark green door, narrow . . . down the stairs."

The bundle of rags shook itself, letting a few wood shavings flutter through the window before Delver closed it, and disappeared. Delver realized that this had been a splendid situation for him for these last few decades, this cellar. Quiet, at the end of a dead-end street; stone floor with a good drain in it and a well of its own, high ceilings which helped when his work became odorous—and the spiders living there among the arches in their tenement of webs didn't seem to be discommoded. Abundant cupboard space for all his supplies, although keeping himself provided with Mercury, Brimstone, Cinnabar, alembics,—and the cost of charcoal! Saltpeter, wax, tin, Arsenicus, Aqua fortis, and Aquaregia! A scandal, the price of things. Existence was becoming even more hand to mouth than ever. Fortunately, Mrs. Strawspinner upstairs was often willing to have him pay his rent by mending her baking pans and molds and pots rather than pay in ready cash, and she was generous with the manure from the cow and horse and chickens she kept for eggs and milk and butter in the tiny stableyard behind her house. He'd have been in trouble all these years, for instance, in keeping Frederick going if she weren't. As it was, he managed, barely, with one odd job and another, and his weekly stint at the palace. He was glad, though, he no longer needed to keep toads—ate their heads off, they did.

The spiders in their webs under the arches, who had been busily stretching their legs and beginning to spin their quota of webs for the day, suddenly curled up into small black polka dots as a whiff of icy air came down the curving stone staircase, followed by the ragged and woebegone small figure that had been hoping for death at the fangs of the wolves outside the cellar window a few moments before.

Drat, the old man thought. Expensive, just like everything else. He'll be needing—things. Like all boys. Soap and shoes—Mr. Delver couldn't recall how many decades had passed since he'd been a boy himself, much less kept one around the place to help out, but surely, surely there was something else boys always needed, if he could only remember.

"Sit down." He pointed to a high, dusty, three-legged stool by the fire. The boy scrambled up, hugging his thin jacket to himself miserably, but Delver was pleased to note that, even shivering with cold and clearly starving—ah, *that* was it, boys needed *food*, just like Frederick, but boys ate every day, all the time—the lad had an interest in things, was peering about and down and around and above.

"You an orphan? Wretched enough looking to be one." Delver was circling around the stool, rubbing his beard and looking at what he could see of the lad beneath the straw in his hair and the rags on his feet and the wood shavings spilling out his cuffs. "You smell of dead leaves, old newspapers, you are woefully stained and soiled, you have more bones than skin, I'll be bound, and I suppose you are fearfully hungry all the time?"

"Yessir," the boy squeaked.

"Perfect." Delver threw open a creaking door that opened off one of the many low dark arches in the corners of the cellar, and disappeared for a moment, making abundant scuffling noises inside. He reappeared, dragging an ancient chest bound in bronze behind him, and under one arm a heavy leather tome with an iron clasp.

Producing a key from an inner pocket in his old leather robe, he unlocked the tome and, placing it on a weighty lectern, began riffling through its pages, peering up from time to time at the boy.

"Alabaster — Antimony — Argentum — Arsenicus — come too far—" He flipped the crackling pages back. "Ah, here we are!" He looked up over his spectacles, placing his finger at the top of a page. "Apprentices."

He began reading aloud, more to himself than to the boy. " 'Apprentices: The first Qualification is that an Apprentice be Grateful.' Are you Grateful? If not, you should think about it. Saved you from freezing to death, didn't I?"

"Oh, yes, sir."

"Very well. Grateful. 'The Second Qualification is that an Apprentice Have No Alternative.' Have you, boy? An Alternative? Such as a Distant Relative who might take you in, or a Benevolent Patron— other than myself, of course—lurking somewhere waiting to befriend you? Hmmm? By the way, have you a name?"

"Andrew, sir, and no, I don't think I *do* have an Alternative." Andrew went on to explain about his pappy, and Thumble, and the wandering happy life of Thomas the Tinker & Son until the avalanche. Mr. Delver rocked back and forth on his heels, looking more and more pleased.

"Splendid. You're utterly bereft. SPLENDID! No Family, no cash, no coffins equals NO ALTERNATIVE! Now, for the Third Qualification. 'An Apprentice Must be Eager'!" He looked doubtfully over the rim of his glasses. "Tell me, *are* you Eager?"

Andrew had no idea what to say, or what all this was about, but it seemed a good idea to be polite. "Oh, yes, very." However, even to him it didn't sound *very* eager.

"Just as I thought," and the old man slammed the book shut, releasing a vast cloud of dust. "Well, you're at least eager to *sound* eager, which is more than most can manage, I can tell you. Zeal—well, Zeal, if it comes at all, comes later. Very well, I'll take you on."

"Thank you, sir, but as what?"

"As what? As my Apprentice, of course." He seized a candle stump and, flinging open the door of a cupboard next to the large, low fireplace, peered in and revealed a long, wide shelf therein. "You'll sleep there, my boy. It's warm and if you're homesick you can close the door and pretend it's one of Mr. Grundage's coffins," he snickered, shuffling back across the floor. Andrew noticed he was wearing one soft leather boot and one fur-lined slipper; the old leather robe came down to his ankles and had bits of fleece lining poking out of innumerable small tears, burn holes, and seams; it had numerous pockets and added to these were various pouches and wallets pinned or laced on any old whichway. His head was completely covered by a brimmed leather hat with long fur lappets covering his ears.

Delver pried the lid of the trunk open and, rummaging deep inside, drew out a large sheet of parchment that crackled with age as he unrolled it.

"Here we are—come over to the table—these were my own Articles of Indenture; parchment's very costly these days, so's my time, so we'll just scratch out my name at the top and put yours in. Perfectly legal, conditions haven't changed in hundreds of years. You *can* read, I hope? Good, good. Well, here we are: Tasks, Responsibilities, Hours. Pumping, of course, any fool can do that, grinding, working the bellows, puddling and stirring and soldering?"

"Oh, yessir, I did all that with my pappy, and he taught me brazing and bellowing, chopping wood and making charcoal, smelting and sawing, soldering and silver-lining too!"

"Thought so, but don't brag. Now. Sorting, sieving, straining, measuring—a bit more skilled, we'll have to see how you do as time goes on. You must learn to coagulate amalgams, distill liquors, elixirs, tinctures from sedimented solutions simmering in aludels, for instance. Tell the difference between pottles, pecks, and pouces, mutchkins, and minims, drams and firkins and pipes, a tun from a tub and both from a vat. Well, as I said, that's for later. Now you read the dratted thing—must get that Brimstone on the boil again, three times three—" He scurried over to the crucible on the floor and put it back on the round stone furnace under the window while Andrew read on.

It seemed he was obliged to stay for seven years, learn the old man's trade—and what was it, Andrew wondered?—would not be held responsible for breakage, nor required to work on Sundays. In return, he would be housed, clothed, and fed—his mouth began to water—and could only be beaten, birched, or caned by the old man himself. If his father had been alive to pay the old man a sum of money for his apprenticeship, and if Andrew died during the seven years, the money was not refundable. Well, Andrew thought, all in all it seemed just about the same life as he'd lived with Pappy, except that Pappy traveled in the wagon and this old man seemed to be pretty wrapped up in his cellar. So he signed his name, Andrew, with a dripping quill pen, and as the old man signed at the bottom next to his name, Andrew learned he was apprenticed to P. C. Delver, Adept and Venerable, and that the charge on Delver's signet ring, which he pressed into a large blob of purple sealing wax, was a flat cap with a brim, and feathered wings on each side of the crown.

"There now—you've been Hermetically sealed! Heh, heh!" tittered Delver, pointing at the wax. "Sign of Hermes, patron something or other . . . forget." A large cauldron hanging in the fireplace chose

that moment to emit a belch and burble, c
Delver to rush forward with a beakerful of ¿
fluid which he began adding to the cauldron, na
ing over his shoulder to Andrew. "See to your..,
lad—your garb is lamentable, by the way—should be
an old ham my sister sent me a year or so ago down
in that trunk, and before that a cheese. Old mother
hen, she is—socks, woollies, lives six countries away
but always sending me things to eat or wear and
knows full well I don't— Get along now, I expect
you to scurry—"

The mention of a ham, however old and foreign,
did indeed send Andrew scurrying, and sure enough
he found a cheese too in the trunk. He almost mis-
took it for a millstone, so old and heavy it was, and
the ham was an unpromising dull gray. But when it
was sliced it fell away from the skin in rosy pink
slices with rims of fat all around. Inside its rind the
cheese was ripe and soft as butter. As he munched,
Andrew heard Delver muttering more to himself than
to him as he bent over the cauldron.

"I expect I ate too, once—can't recall. Herring?
Is there something called herring? And porridge, or
gruel? Bowls with spoons, I do remember that." He
threw a pinch of a glittering powder from a pouch at
his belt into the cauldron. It flared and a tall blue
flame shot up the chimney.

Deciding it was better not to stuff himself too
full after a fast, and that if Delver himself didn't eat
he probably didn't keep a kitchen, Andrew resolved
to make the ham and cheese last as long as possible.

He found a tattered but warm fur-lined green velvet jacket that fit, more or less, if he rolled the sleeves halfway up, and a pair of shoes that, pulled on over his own boots with a pair of thick socks and tufts of old fur in between, made his feet quite warm if a bit less nimble. All in all, things had improved a great deal in the last hour. Whoever Delver was, abrupt, querulous, and imperious, still and all he had a warm cellar he was sharing, a cupboard shelf which needed only a sackful of straw to be a comfortable bed, and an occupation that surely would be interesting if Andrew could only find out what it was.

"Ruination!" Delver was squinting up through one of the windows; Andrew could see the sun had gone under and snowflakes were falling, serious big ones. "If the sun's gone I'll have to shift the order of procedure entirely—or wait, perhaps I'll just put everything on the back grate and get a few mundane things out of the way. Palace's been nattering after me for the King's horoscope all week—good a day as any to get that bit of trivia out of the way. Give me a hand here, lad."

Andrew was helping Delver arrange the pots, alembics, crucibles, retorts in suitable places near the fire where they would keep just warm enough but not too warm, when there was a mighty crash from overhead. Dust, cobwebs, and bits of loose mortar fell on the floor; the spiders rolled themselves philosophically up into polka dots again.

"Oh, drat, drat, drat!" Delver coughed through the dust. "I believe I neglected to mention that one

of the first duties of an Apprentice is to KEEP PEO-
PLE OUT OF MY HAIR!"

"Yessir."

"In this case, my esteemed landlady. From the
sound of that, she'll be sending down in a minute for
some assistance; nip up there, Andrew, and give her a
hand—introduce yourself, keep her from coming
down— Oh, the frustration of it all, just as my life
work is coming to fruition!"

"Yessir, but—"

"But what? Hop it, I say!"

"I don't rightly know how to introduce myself
unless I know what I'm apprenticed to you for,
d'you see? I don't know what you *do*."

A terrible cold chill filled the room. "*Do?*"
Delver drew himself up so that his velvet cap with
the long earlaps seemed to sweep the ceiling.

"Yessir. Do. To use me as your Apprentice—all
those things—pumping and mixing and grinding—"
Andrew's voice faded away timidly.

"I do not *do*." Delver's eyes became terrible. "I
am."

"Am what, sir?"

"An Alchemist!"

Chapter II

The very air around the old man crackled, sizzled, and then subsided. Andrew, who had unthawed enough and eaten enough to have his wits back, realized that somehow or other he had said quite the wrong thing, waited a moment before he answered. "Oh, of course."

"No 'of course' about it. *How* old are you?"

"Eleven, sir."

"Perhaps that excuses it. I'll blame it on your youth. To work." He seized a large leather-bound roll of papers and, heading himself for a distant dark archway, closed like all the others with heavy low doors, pointed at the stone stairs Andrew had come down. "Up the stairs, outside, and up the stoop—Strawspinner's Sweets and Savories." Delver disappeared into the gloom.

The gold-bordered sign of the shop swung violently in the snowy wind as Andrew knocked sharply on the door. It must have been unlocked, for the door swung open, a little bell tinkling from the top. Stepping in quickly, he felt that with one breath he'd gained ten pounds, the air was so full of vanilla, mushrooms, cinnamon, cheeses, almond, chocolate, onion, sassafras, butter, molasses, mincemeat, sausages, peppermint. The little shop had a counter on each side of the door, one with glass shelves full of rolls, tarts—both meat and sweet—muffins, turnovers, biscuits, gingerbread. The other counter was topped with a row of round glass jars, each filled with nuts, raisins, currants, candies, taffies dark and light.

"C'n I help you?" He jumped; the voice was close but he couldn't see anyone. Then one of the glass jars moved—not a glass jar of taffy at all, but a girl's round head, with taffy-colored hair exactly the color of the contents of the jars on either side.

"Oh. Well, I came—was sent, you see, to help you. I'm Andrew, Mr. Delver's new Apprentice. We heard a crash—" He looked into raisin-brown eyes set in toasted-biscuit skin with freckles.

"—and he sent you up to keep me or Maam from coming down and bothering him." The girl grinned. "Yep, you *can* help. I knocked over the big candy kettle; come back in the kitchen." And she led the way through a small door in the rear. A large copper kettle, one of the biggest Andrew had ever seen, was lying on the floor. He ran his hands over it knowledgeably, and looked up. "Well, it's all right, no cracks or anything."

"You sound like you know what you're talking about." She stood looking down at him, hands on hips, brown all over in dress, boots, and even a tan apron, very square and sturdy.

"My pappy was a tinker—" and as they righted the heavy kettle and set it back on the stove he told the girl of his fortune in the past few weeks. She had pulled a pan of agonizingly aromatic currant muffins between them at the table, and they were both eating away.

"Hmmm. I never knew *my* father at all. Well, I suppose you could have ended up worse than with old Delver—have another muffin—he can be pretty prickly sometimes, but it usually doesn't add up to much. Just as well, really, that you pawned your hand bell. If you'd had it with you now, I bet Delver'd have melted it down quicker'n quick. This way you stand *some* chance of getting it back if you ever earn any money."

"Well, I'd like to have it, you know; it's the only thing left of my pappy's after the avalanche." And he put his cup and muffin down, lowering his eyes.

"Finish your muffin. My name's Sassie, Sassie Strawspinner. Maam's out with the van making the morning deliveries." Andrew, as he blinked back his tears, saw her cutting her own last muffin in two and putting half on his plate.

"Listen, Sassie, why would Mr. Delver have melted down my old bell? And he got all fussed and crackly when I asked him what he did. Pappy never told me anything about Alchemists, you see, and it's going to be hard to be his Apprentice if I don't know what it is he does."

"Well, it's like this far as *I* can understand." Sassie took the top off a pot of dark, rich jam and pushed it toward Andrew after helping herself. "Alchemists, you see, are people who try to make gold —make it, not mine it or find it in a river or earn it —by taking base metals, like lead and iron or copper, y'know, and removing all the impurities. Well to do that they first have to make something called a Philosopher's Stone, but don't ask me what it is or how. They need that to purify the metals; I do know that. They grind the Stone down and make an elixir or something of it and combine it with base metals, like your bell f'rinstance, and somehow or other they make gold. Takes years and years, Maam says, and she doesn't believe in it anyway."

"She doesn't?"

"Nope. Says if he could, why does he always pay the rent in silver, and shuffle around looking poor as a church mouse? Although she did tell me when he first rented the cellar from her he told her 'It takes gold to make gold, Mrs. S., and you'll have to be content with silver and copper.' He's been here years and years—long before I was born—Maam says he came from well over four countries away and was an old man even then. But he's harmless," she said, standing up and gathering up the empty muffin tin and their plates and cups, "and gets by doing odd jobs, knife sharpening and odd bits of metalwork, repairing things and so on, and he gets to do the King's horoscope every week, so he must be pretty good at that, anyway."

"Who's good at what and who have we here, I say!" Sassie's mother, who had come in through the back door with a gust of cold air, looked more like a pecan than Andrew had thought possible. A little brown nut of a woman, her cloak and hood waxed so heavily against wind and rain it looked like a smooth nutshell, and her face a congregation of friendly brown wrinkles.

"Delver has an Apprentice, hmm? Well, welcome, young man. He's going to need some company; whole town's up in arms and of course nitwits like old Grundage, and some of the coarser elements from the palace, and Samson overt' the inn are yelping about black magic and what does Delver *really* do down in my cellar, with blue and green lights at night and horrible stinks from time to time. No worse'n Samson's stableyard smells *all* the time, but you know how fools are—have to blame somebody for the new lake and Delver's such a loner he's the easiest to pick on."

"New lake, ma'am?" Andrew asked, as Mrs. Strawspinner began peeling off her hood and cloak and pouring herself a cup of coffee.

"Andrew just got to town, Maam," and Sassie told his story briefly as she got the cream jug for her mother.

"I see—the great avalanche, hmm. Well now, lad, that *is* a tragic misfortune and there's no gainsaying it. You must just get through your grief as best

21

you can, like I had to when Sassie's pa was took from us by the fever and she no more than a babe. But it might help some to think that if your pappy was anything like other tinkers I've known, that was a good way for him to go, Andrew. They're a restless lot, tinkers are, and this was quick and fast, just like his life was.

"Well, as I was saying then, yes, t'other morning —day before yesterday? no matter—whole town woke up and found a huge lake in the valley beneath the town, where the old stone and thistle field and piddly little pond had been."

"You mean the lake wasn't always there? I *thought* things looked different but I was so shook up about Pappy—"

"Of course you were, Andrew. Nope, a new lake, and frozen smooth as glass, stretching to the edge of every single mountain around! And this morning it had risen eighteen inches! Good thing it's winter and all the folks have their cattle in, otherwise they'd be frozen in it too! Speaking of livestock, git your jacket on, Sass, and unharness old Raisin for me 'n put the van away, child. Andrew can give you a hand if you want."

The small cobbled stableyard behind Mrs. Strawspinner's house backed up against a high stone wall. "That's the back of the palace grounds beyond it. If you want to look at the lake, climb up to the top; you can see it over the top of Maam's roof." Andrew found toeholds easily in the massive stone blocks of the wall, and soon was straddled across the top, looking back down across the town's chimneys and roofs, the winding streets of the little town. Yes, there beyond the town wall and the main gate he'd come through days ago, a vast sheet of black ice covered the whole countryside. Tops of scrubby trees stuck up like young twigs, and in places the wind caught drifted snow and formed shapes that for a lingering moment resembled dragons, demons, and ominous skeletal fingers.

Turning to go down and help Sassie, he saw the glittering palace turrets and rooftops on the other side, flags fluttering and smoke coming from gilt chimneys. "You can get a real look if you go round the town and look through the palace gates," Sassie called, hurrying into the little stable with Raisin's still-warm harness before the leather stiffened and cracked; Raisin followed her with no hesitation.

Andrew joined them and grabbed a handful of warm, dry straw and stood on Raisin's other side, helping Sassie rub her down. The sweat had almost turned to ice outside. There was a brindle cow in the next stall, a goat and ducks and chickens, a beehive. "Maam won't cook with nothing but the freshest eggs and butter," Sassie said proudly, measuring out a handsome mangerful of oats for Raisin before they shut the stable door and left the animals inside, warm and protected. She clambered up into the tiny, gaily painted van which bore the legend "Strawspinner's Sweets and Savories" and a small crest underneath which was lettered "By Appointment to His Majesty, King Oliver the Eleventh, and the Royal Household."

She handed down armfuls of empty baking tins, molds, and racks to Andrew.

"There's the manure heap, when Delver sends you up for some—and he will, too; don't know what he needs it for, but help yourself."

"Thanks. Do you think I could have some straw to make a mattress?" He explained about the bare-shelved cupboard that was to be his bed.

"Oh, sure." And she clattered the empty baking tins into the shed room behind the kitchen while Andrew stuffed two empty feed bags with clean, sweet clover and alfalfa. He was about to call out to Sassie to thank her maam for him, not wanting to drag the mattress and pillow through the shop, when Mrs. Strawspinner herself stuck her head out the shed door.

"Come up again soon's he's no need of you, Andrew; we can always trade a bite or two for a helping hand. And now your stomach's full, here's food for thought: If I were you I'd stay low for a bit. . . . Town's all het up and nervous, what with poor crops all summer and heavy snows and now that frozen lake . . . not a good climate for strangers, not at all."

Chapter III

The note propped on the heavy lectern in the cellar was unreadable at first until Andrew saw the small looking glass of burnished bronze leaning beside it. He held up the note and saw that it was only written backwards, in a very small, crabbed hand, and not after all in a cypher or foreign language.

> Stoke athanor straw keep crucible at fume alembic at fizzle grind Orpiment mortar UNDER NO CIRCUMSTANCES FEED FREDERICK!

All very well, but who or what was Frederick, and more important, what was an athanor? Alembic? Crucible he knew, of course. His pappy had had a small kettle-shaped vessel for melting down tin and solder and such things. Timidly, Andrew opened the great iron-bound tome and began to read. "Athanor: The brick furnace of Alchemists, generally round and stoked from below with various fuels according to purpose." He followed his finger to the next page. "Alembic: The apparatus of Distillation, best made of glass, next best of copper or a combination of the two" and so on.

Hoping that using the tome would come under the category of an Apprentice being Eager, Andrew stoked the athanor, which was under the window that had kept him from freezing to death, with the neatly stacked faggots of tarred straw that were piled beside it, and saw that the crucible continued a steady fume. The alembic in the fireplace was fizzling to perfection; there seemed to be nothing needed there for the time being. Andrew drew a bucket of water from the well in the corner and scrubbed out his cupboard before putting his mattress and pillow in; he had seen a cobweb or two he didn't wish to have as bedfellows.

Still no sign of Delver; a scrubbing broom in a corner made him think it might be enterprising to attend to the floor, so with more water, heated and soapy, he went to it with a will, the double boots on his feet keeping his toes dry, and the floor drain carrying away the dust and dirt of years. One spot near an arch—he didn't, somehow, want to go too near those arches, even with their stout wooden doors—dried a bit lighter. Had he scrubbed harder there, or was it just a different kind of stone? Before he could tell, he heard voices coming down through the window he had left open to help dry the floor. It was so warm in the basement from the huge fireplace and his own exertions that the crisp knife blade of winter air was actually welcome now.

"Scandal, that's wot it is; sure's sure 'tis Black Magic he's be doin' there. . . ."

"Or else why the lake where t'old pond was?

Oh, he's been working at it fer years, sez I, all them evil doin's—"

Andrew looked up; he could see two pairs of thickly booted feet standing on the sidewalk, stomping slightly on the snowy cobbles.

"Wouldn't come round here a'tall if it weren't for the Sweets and Savories—best lardy cake in the country, but the wife do say not to get any friendlier now with old Mrs. Strawspinner, nor that girl of hers neither; anybody who'd rent their cellar to a Black Magus like that—"

"Thass right, and my daughter's lass, wot's a maid at the palace, do tell Prime Minister Bogardus be tryin' to get King Oliver to stop his order from Strawspinner's too, but so far old King's sweet tooth got the better of his judgment. If I were king I'd throw 'em all in that lake, thass what—"

The voices drifted away, full of ignorance and hatred and fear. Andrew shivered and closed the window with the long pole that dangled from it. He'd rather smell a few fumes of Brimstone than hear that kind of talk. I wonder if Mr. Delver knows, he thought, emptying the last of the scrub water down the floor drain and watching it swirl down and away. Round and round—horrors! He'd forgotten to grind the whatever it was in the mortar!

It was on one of the sturdier tables, and needed to be, for the mortar and pestle were made of solid agate, the mortar as big as a dishpan and the pestle the size of Andrew's arm. He brought another candle over to be sure he ground as finely as he could; it was hard to tell what the substance was, but it was as beautiful a yellow pile of crystalline dust as he'd ever seen by the time he had finished pounding and swirling and grinding and stirring.

"Orpiment" he found in the tome on the lectern. "Aurum Pigmentum, or King's Gold." Could *this* be some of the gold the Alchemist was making? Oh, it was so beautiful, but alas, when he lifted a handful of the dust, it didn't seem very heavy at all—surely gold dust would weigh importantly in the hand? Brushing the last grain back into the mortar, he returned to the tome and pulled up a stool. "Aurum Hispanicum—" Golly! "Take red copper, of human blood from a red-haired man (*Hominis Rufi!* Delver had written backwards in the margin, crossly), ashes of mature Basilisks, vinegar—" Basilisks! Andrew thought, his blood racing as he flipped to the B's.

"Produce Basilisks in this matter: See to a subterranean chamber, stone-floored and secretly entered, or as best to it as may be. Take two cocks, well aged of fifteen years, fatten well, sparing them nothing of nourishment. Thus their mating will occur; secure the eggs carefully, keeping warm whilst you discard the cocks, they being of no further use save for a stewpot, gaining you favor with a neighbor. Take you then the large toads, one for each egg, you have been keeping, and let the toads hatch the eggs. Feed the toads on bread from fine wheaten loaves during their task. When chicks are hatched, return toads to their cages.

"The chicks which have come forth may run

free until seven days time have passed, when they will begin to grow serpent's tails. CAVEAT: This is the point at which they would burrow into the ground to escape, twere not for the stone floor. Having provided yourself with brazen vessels with copper covers, of a vast size, perforated round with small holes, seize the hatched chicks *by their tails* and, one to a vessel, seal them within hermetically. Bury the vessels in deep mounds of the finest manure in a dark corner; they will nourish for half a year on the sifting dung through the holes. Maturing at six months, uncover and place brazen vessel on fire, reducing the Basilisk within to ashes which unlike live Basilisk are quite harmless. For use, see Aurum Hispanicum, or Spanish Gold.

"Yaiii!" Andrew yelped as a hand touched his shoulder; the light was dim and day was done. "Oh, golly, Sassie—"

"Gee, what're you so wrapped up in you didn't even hear me come down?" She put a package on the table and came over to the lectern and started reading the entry Andrew showed her.

"Wow . . . no wonder you yelped!" she said as she finished it, turning the page. "Hey, there's *more* —come on, get another candle; you're in my light!"

"N.B.: Basilisks are of extreme danger alive and outside their vessels. A look from one turns the viewed to stone immediately. They can crush rocks with their bodies; Basilisks are viewable, and this with much danger, only by means of a looking glass over one's shoulder, taking great care the Basilisk does not see you.

"Basilisks may be kept successfully and safely, if not needed immediately, by feeding twice yearly (crumbs suffice) at summer and winter solstices and at the same time renewing dung as required for deep burial."

And there was another mirror-writing margin note in Delver's hand which Andrew read out to Sassie. "*Deep* burial, or the scraping of their scales *infernally* noisy against brass."

Andrew wondered which of their faces was whiter, his or Sassie's.

"Golly! They look like a cross between a dragon and a rooster!" His thumb was next to a picture of a Basilisk, its face turned away.

"Yeah, but they must be *huge*—remember it said to put them in a vessel of *vast size!*" Sassie looked about the cellar quickly.

"Don't worry, I've just scrubbed down the whole place and there's nothing like that around." But Andrew didn't tell Sassie he hadn't been behind the closed-off archways.

"*That's* a relief," Sassie said, taking a deep breath. "Maam wouldn't stand for anything like *that*, for one thing. And *I'd* sure hate to bump into one, even if they do only eat crumbs. Don't want to be turned into a rock the rest of my life."

"Heck, don't worry. We don't know if Mr. Delver even made one, anyway."

Andrew quickly pushed Sassie toward the stairs as they heard the unmistakable shuffle of Delver's slipper and shoe coming from an arched corner, and the clank of a wooden door closing. Sassie nodded, laid her finger against her lips, pointed at the package on the table and at Andrew, and scurried soundlessly up the stairs.

"Hmmm—" Delver said, coming into the light and looking about him, noting the tome open on the lectern at B instead of A where he had left it. He sifted a bit of the ground Orpiment in his fingers, nodded, and tossed his leather-covered roll of papers into a corner. "Bah, horoscopes. Tiresome, tedious— necessary, but tiresome. I see you have extended yourself, young man." He glared at the floor, which looked quite handsome compared to its appearance this morning. "Didn't get right up to the arches, I see? Skimping already, hmm?"

"Well, actually, sir, not knowing as how you might want them all undisturbed, I *didn't* scrub right up to the edge—" But even to Andrew it sounded a poor excuse, especially as Delver was standing right next to the lighter-colored patch of stone which made the rest around it look a bit darker than they really were.

"Didn't think you would—just as well, I expect. Leave 'em alone. Didn't feed Frederick, did you?" He glared under his beetle brows.

"Oh, no, sir. As a matter of fact, I didn't even *see*—Frederick."

"Of course not. Aren't meant to. When you are, you will. Open the trunk; forgot something this morning."

Andrew opened the old trunk again, reminded of the ham and cheese in it that would very likely be his supper, and grateful to the midmorning tuck-in with Sassie and Mrs. Strawspinner.

Delver rummaged around in the trunk, which gave off puffs of dust again, and finally pulled out a curious object of felt and leather, turning it round in his hands thoughtfully as if his mind were very far away in time and place. He gave it a brush on his sleeve and handed it to Andrew.

"Rules say that when an Alchemist becomes an Adept, he must change his own name, and put his Apprentice in a Pointed Hat. Became an Adept so long ago forget now what my other name was—have it written down somewhere, I expect—then I became a Venerable, and got to change the color of my robe. This one's so old it's hard to tell, but I *think* I chose puce—that's right, a rich, handsome puce, bit faded now, could do with a good clean but it's puce all right. Well, should have given you the hat this morning—actually, it was mine when I was an Apprentice. Must ask you not to wear it outside just now; find yourself a rabbit skin or an old sack if you have to—doesn't do to call attention to ourselves just now, town's skittish, be discreet. Hat's a bit unusual." Andrew remembered the horrid gossip of the booted townsmen earlier. No need to tell Delver of that, then. The hat *was* unique, quite pointed and the peak stiffened like an umbrella with wires, and it had a flopping, and somewhat tattered, brim; the whole was covered with suns, moons, runic designs. Andrew was thrilled and put it on immediately. He was dying to show it to Sassie.

"Could I ask a question, sir? I tried to be Eager, and so I found out a little about what an Alchemist does—er, sorry, *is*—but I didn't know about the Adept and Venerable part. Except on your signature this morning."

"Few do. But I see you've been Zealous about your own comfort, though. Contrived a pallet and pillow for your cupboard—drat it, have you let that alembic stop fizzling—no, I suppose you haven't—" Delver was pacing the room, hands behind his back, clearly trying to avoid Andrew's unspoken question that thickened the air.

"What's this object? This unspeakable domestic mess here?" He pointed with a poker at the bundle on the table that Sassie had left behind.

"Oh. Oh, it's something from Mrs. Strawspinner —I think for me, but perhaps for you? Shall I open it, sir?"

"Humph. Get it over with."

Andrew untied the clean checked cloth and spread it out on the table. "Why, it's dinner, sir—potatoes to bake on the fire, and a mushroom tart, a *big* one, and apples, honey, seedcakes!"

"I may retch. Cover it up instantly. Stuff yourself at a suitable time if you must, but not in front of me."

"May I wear the hat while I'm eating, sir?" Delver groaned inside; he was clearly going to have to explain, and the Rules *did* say he was obliged to teach the quodling—Masters just as rigidly bound as Apprentices—might as well get it over with.

"Very well. V-e-r-y w-e-l-l. Question one. An Adept is One Who Has Attained. Attained the First Step, the Quest for the Materia Prima, the Philosopher's Stone. Two: Venerable follows and may be applied to an Adept who has mastered the Second Step, the Magnum Opus. To you, lad, gold."

Andrew gulped. "The Stone—the Philosopher's Stone—and gold! You have!" He tossed his hat in the air in sheer joy; now Delver could leave his cellar, live decently, a rich man—

"What's the cause for rejoicing? Happened a long time ago—so long I can't remember—nothing terribly difficult if one's persistent and inventive and above all, UNINTERRUPTED. That, as I recall, was the hardest—keeping PEOPLE out of my hair—and still is." Delver glared at the checked cloth on the table, as if he knew Sassie had brought it down herself. "Oh, yes, The Stone—which some call the Egg—was laborious, making it, lots of waste and error in time and material. The gold came quite a bit faster, but of course by then I'd mastered most of the instruments and techniques; that helped. My, there was a lot of gold—more than I'd thought of or needed, wasteful, really. Difficult to get rid of, on top of it all, that *was* a bore. Would have been easier to throw it away or spend it or something, I suppose, but that's forbidden. Puts too much emphasis on the thing itself and not the process—that's where gold defeats more Alchemists than anything in history, the temptation to stop at the gold and live rich and high off the hog. Speaking of hog—"

Andrew was just going to ask him if he hadn't spent the gold or given it away, what had he done with it. But Delver was poking at the supper on the table with his staff.

"Eat up, if you really must, and off to bed with you. Heavy work tomorrow. Laundry, if you want to know ahead of time. Starting a new phase and must have clean linen for it. Both of us. Baths and all. Essential."

"Right, sir, but—"

"But, but, but—one more question and THAT'S ALL!"

"If you've made a Philosopher's Stone, and then gone on and made gold from base metals, what else is there left to do? The Third Step? What is it?" Andrew turned the pointed hat politely round in his hands, looking up over it shyly at the fierce, bristling old man.

"The Third Step? The Third and Final Step? And on your FIRST DAY as my Apprentice you ask that? And expect an *answer?* Stuff and nonsense. Literally. Stuff yourself and stop the nonsense." Delver huffed off into one of the gloomy corners, tittering into his beard. Andrew, glad enough to tuck into his supper, put the potatoes on the hot coals to roast and resigned himself to waiting for further teaching.

Snuggled up in his cupboard later, which smelt a bit of mice but more of the sweet alfalfa and clover and hay in his mattress, and a bit of the tail end of the mushroom tart he had under his pillow in case he had bad dreams and woke up in the night—Pappy had always let him—Andrew fell asleep quickly, warm and full for the first time in days.

No dreams of frozen lakes, dark and rising, lost or hidden gold, Basilisks or the blood of red-haired men troubled his dreams that night, or in the nights to come during the next week or so. He was far too tired not to go to sleep instantly when his head touched his pillow, and far too interested during the day to be bored.

He and Delver managed their ritual baths and clean linen, and then Delver proceeded to cast his own horoscope. "Always at the beginning of a new phase of work, boy—nonsense, perhaps, but good insurance." Apparently finding the results auspicious, Delver pinned it to the wall and set to work with a will. For several days Andrew manned the bellows, lugged charcoal in from the fuel storage bin under one of the arches, while Delver blew enormously complicated glass vessels and instruments of great beauty. "Reason the glass is so clear, like looking through a star, you might say, is that I went to the sand pits myself just as the moon was increscent last summer—sand taken during a decrescent moon gives you cloudy glass, no matter what you do."

Delver was apparently quite proud of his technique; Andrew wished he could take the time to try it a bit himself, knowing nothing of this skill. He picked up what tips he could, but at the end the main thing he seemed to have learned was that the way an Alchemist did something seemed to be as important, if not more important, than what he did. And however it was done was the most inconvenient, complicated, ritualistic and bloody-minded way possible. Some things had to be done at night, others on sunny days; clouds compelled cessation of certain distillations, while the phase of the moon encouraged other coagulations to occur in copper retorts and flasks. All very puzzling. Once upon a while Delver would be more aware of Andrew's presence than other times, and mutter something like "To an Alchemist, Andrew, All Else is Secondary—see you don't forget it."

Or: "They say we seek facts at the expense of wisdom. Hah. Little do they know."

And once: "Every Alchemist has to start over for himself. Much is written down, most of it lies to mislead one's colleagues—do it myself, tee hee—but what's written down is of little use anyway when you get around to needing it.

"Alchemists do their best work in countries other than their own. You'll have to move on in seven years time, my boy, if you're going on with this gig—"

Occasionally the cellar got a bit confining, like working inside a hard-boiled egg, what with the fumes and fizzling and flamings that were going on, but Delver, fortunately for Andrew, occasionally ran out of essentials, which meant that Andrew was given enough errands in the town to keep exercised and well aired. The air outside was wonderfully, amazingly cold and crisp as a hard apple.

Sassie would run into him from time to time, giving him a lift on the delivery van if she were going his way. More often than not her mother would have placed a "leftover" just inside the green door under the stoop, so what with the stream of goodies from above, and Mr. Delver's ham and cheese, Andrew was picking up in weight and color and quite enjoying what there was to enjoy.

The great frozen lake was always there, an astonishment and curiosity to Sassie and Mrs. Strawspinner, and an object of some actual beauty to Andrew, who had not known the town without it. But to most of the townsmen, it was a mysterious threat, dark, troubling, unutterably evil.

One afternoon Andrew had come away from the blacksmith empty-handed; there had been no spare anvil for loan or purchase, not even for ready money, to replace the one that Mr. Delver had cracked the evening before. Even though Andrew had seen at least half a dozen new ones in the back of the shop, with the prices clearly marked. But not for the mysterious Delver, the blacksmith's attitude clearly said as he uttered a curse against the evil eye and slammed the bolt shut after Andrew.

Sassie happened along then, the empty van clattering and Raisin clopping on the cobbles. She slowed down long enough for Andrew to hop up beside her.

"Got a minute, Andrew?"

"Guess so, sure. Hey, where'd you get that long

scratch on the side of the van; it's scraped right through the paint work!"

"Oh, one of the street urchins—a bunch of them, really—were waiting when I came out this morning. Threw stones and sticks and all that. Funny, their folks spread gossip about us and what old man Delver's doing in our cellar and the black lake and all that, but they still buy or beg all Maam's cooking. What *I* want to do now is see how a frozen lake can keep rising the way this one's doing—that's half of what scares people so much, I'll bet."

She turned Raisin down toward the town's gate in the old low wall; they left the paved road for the somewhat spongier hummocks of the rim of the stone pastureland. "Whoa-up!" Sassie jumped down and flung a blanket over the little horse, and she and Andrew squished to the water's edge. And water it was for a few inches, before the black, ominous ice began. They stuck their fingers in it; Andrew thought he wouldn't exactly want to swim in it, but it certainly wasn't *all* solid ice.

He picked up a stone the size of a hefty potato and, winding up as best he could, threw it as far as possible. The ice was thick all right, the stone didn't star or even scratch the surface, but skidded on away out of sight.

"No wonder Maam's gonna take a day off soon and get out her old skates—looks wonderful!" Sassie was glowing with the cold air. "Says she'll keep store for me the next day and let me go; think old Delver might let you off? Can you skate?"

"Sure I can. Well, I can ask him. I'm supposed to get every Sunday off, you know. Boy, I'd think everybody in town'd be out having a wonderful time."

"You just don't know these people, Andrew; until some sort of explanation comes down from the palace they're like sheep about everything. Can't think for themselves at all, or won't; they're so used to that Prime Minister Bogardus telling them whether or not the sun's shining. And on top of it all, it was a bad summer for their crops, rainy and cold, and by fall all the good farmland and pastures on the mountains were just hills of mud; Maam says that always makes for avalanches and we've had some—well, you know that. But, no, it 'tisn't a good winter, with lots of folks hungry. Come on; we'd better get back."

Chapter IV

King Oliver the Eleventh rose from his breakfast of plum muffins dripping with butter and cherry jam, coddled eggs and grilled pheasant; he took a bunch of royal purple hothouse grapes from the sideboard as he left the dining room. Really, he thought, that woman, what's-her-name, in the town is the most superb muffin maker. As usual, his Prime Minister, Bogardus, was waiting outside in the broad hallway.

"Good morning, Your Majesty," he said, with a deep bow.

"Morning, 'gardus." Oliver bustled down the hallway to his second-best throne room where he spent most of his days. The large state throne room was very difficult to heat and the throne itself excruciatingly uncomfortable; the little room was full of the King's hobbies, didn't need to be dusted and tidied all the time, and was warm as toast.

"Tell me, Bogardus," the King said, looking out the double windows to the rear palace gates, "why are all those people standing around the back gates like that every day? They know perfectly well I never go out, not even as far as a balcony, in such cold weather. What do they want?"

Bogardus drew a lace-edged kerchief from his sleeve and flourished it under his nose, as if even inside the palace he could smell the offending rabble. "Hunger, my lord. We give them each a dish of gruel daily. You may recall their summer harvest was blasted by rot and rain and hailstorms. Many of them lost cattle in the avalanches this winter. Chickens frozen to death and so forth."

"Gruel? Is that all the treasury can afford? Should think we could do a bit better than that— fling in a few raisins, hmm?"

"It's much more than they're accustomed to, I assure you, Your Majesty. Raisins would only confuse them."

"Raisins never confuse *me*, Bogardus. Always cheer me up, as a matter of fact." Oliver finished the last of his grapes and sat down grumpily on his small padded throne. "What's *in* the treasury these days, anyway? Haven't been down for a look-see for donkey's years. Damp old vault, isn't it?"

"Exceedingly damp, and cold, sire. If Your Majesty wishes to have the crown jewels brought up, he has only to say."

"Oh, I know that. No need for them this winter. Nobody coming or going, no state visits, ambassadors, balls, banquets. Dull. What's the news on that infernal lake, by the way?"

"Up another four inches this morning, my lord. The people are becoming more and more alarmed."

"All the more reason to beef up the dole, then, Bogardus. Raisins. Have the kitchen fling in a sackful of raisins in their gruel from now on. Nothing like raisins for keeping mobs quiet. Now, what *shall* I do this morning?"

"Your stamp collection, Sire?"

"No, no, bores me to tears. Finished work on that last clock you brought me yesterday; tricky job but it runs like—clockwork! Heh, heh! Oh, the tedium of being king. Aren't there some laws I should pass, or proclamations I should make? Something about the lake perhaps?"

"I've taken care of all that for you, Sire. Such matters are the ultimate in tedium, I assure you."

"Humph. Suppose so." One of the King's clocks began to strike; the others followed with chime upon chime. And old Delver isn't due here for my horoscope and astrology lesson for another hour, the King thought. He scratched his head, yawned, reached for a pen and wrote a postcard to his sister who had married the king of a neighboring realm.

"I know!" He sat up suddenly. "Just the thing. I *haven't* been down to the treasury vault for years. Send for my fur boots and woollies, Bogardus. I've a mind to go down and count some coins for a while. Stop in the kitchens on my way back and tell 'em about the raisins, too."

"Your Majesty, I strongly recommend against visiting the vaults in such weather. The damp is appalling underfoot and the temperature is worse!"

"What do I have furs for, and ermine robes?

Some of those emeralds the Chinese ambassador brought me were very pretty—like to see 'em again. And all those boxes and boxes of coins . . ."

"I'll have the jewels brought up directly, Sire."

"No, no." The King was struggling into his ermine robes, his valet stuffing his fat little feet into great fur-lined boots of royal purple suede. "I want to see it all together—the riches of the realm. Cheer me up on such a gray day."

"In that case, perhaps Your Majesty will excuse me . . . Other duties . . ."

"Nonsense, come along, Bogardus. Need your key to begin with, lost mine years ago. You know more than anyone about where some of the treasures come from anyway. We must begin a catalogue; there was a whole coffer of pearls my father got from someone in return for a dukedom. We should bring them up—bad for pearls to live in the dark."

Footmen carrying torches led them down winding stairs into the depths of the palace, along a crudely paved tunnel leading far into the darkest, deepest, most ancient reaches of the palace's vast foundation.

"By Jove, I'd forgotten the old dungeons. Used back in Great-great-grandfather Dagobert's time, weren't they? Those grills were certainly built to last!" They were passing a series of small, dark cells, filled with cobwebs and dust, an occasional icicle hanging from the ceilings. "Ah, here we are!" The King was rubbing his hands together in anticipation. "I remember it now! Came here with my daddy, Oliver the Tenth, for birthday treats when I was little!" The great wrought-iron grillwork doors of the treasure vault were before them. Bogardus stood silently, wrapped in dark, sable-lined cloaks. "Come along, come along, Bogardus. Open it up, man!"

Slowly the Prime Minister detached a massive key from the chain of state which rested on his shoulders, and inserted it in the lock. The doors swung open toward them. "Keep 'em well oiled, don't you? I was hoping for a nice ghostly squeak!" Oliver tittered, bounding into the vault, the footmen directly behind him with their torches.

"What! Bogardus, what's this? What's this?" The vault, arched in the torchlight directly over their heads, was lined with shelves, bins, great leather coffers and caskets resting on padded platforms to keep them from the damp floor. King Oliver remembered how the torchlight would glitter and glint with the dazzlement of gold in all of them, gold coins, bars, ingots, crystal jars of gold dust, bins of jewels.

There was nothing there. Nothing except the crown jewels—the Crown, Scepter, Ring, Spur, Buckle, Mace, Orb, Garter—glinting sad and lonely in their glass case, awaiting another coronation. The shelves and bins and coffers were clean swept, not even a cobweb. Off in a lone corner Oliver found a bag of coins, in a casket a few more, but the rest of the royal treasure had completely disappeared.

"But it was full!" wailed the King. "It was a marvel of gold and silver and gems! Bogardus, what happened?"

"Sire, I—" and the Prime Minister held his hands out emptily, as bewildered as the little monarch.

It spoke well for the stern training of the footmen that they did not flinch or shudder as, quite unexpectedly, a row of empty shelves began to move in the light of the flickering torches they held. Moved, swung out, and from the dark behind them stepped a tall, hunched old man wearing a leather cap with fur lappets over his ears and half-moon spectacles on his nose, a bunch of papers rolled up under his arm.

"Delver!" squealed the King.

"Delver! Guards, guards!" roared Bogardus over his shoulder. Guards came running down the tunnel and into the treasury. "Seize him!" and they grabbed the old man by each arm.

"What's all this? What's— Good morning, Your Majesty." Delver peered over his glasses. "Oh, yes, good morning, your Prime Minister. Didn't expect to see you here."

"I can imagine." Bogardus pulled himself up tall. "How long have you been removing the King's gold from the treasury, you thieving, fraudulent old so-called Alchemist?"

"Stealing his gold? Whatever do you mean? What would I want to do that for? I just come to the palace this way through an old tunnel I found— warmer than going outside in the snow—been using this passage for some time now, very useful—goes right from my cellar under the palace wall and comes out here. I say, could these fellows let me go? Don't like being touched, you know."

"Pity." Bogardus stroked his mustache as he answered sarcastically. "So here we have a so-called Alchemist who has insinuated himself into the King's favor by casting fraudulent horoscopes. Oh, no doubt of it, Your Majesty; didn't all of them say 'auspicious' and 'splendid opportunity' for anything you wanted to do? Hmm? You got told what you wanted to hear, I wager. And during the process," he continued, turning back to Delver, "well paid as you were, old reprobate, you discover a way in and out of the treasure vault and make off with the gold and jewels bit by bit. We'll have your head for this. Passing yourself off as an Alchemist and Astrologer. You're naught but a common thief!"

"Not so! Not so!" Delver stamped one foot, which was about all the movement the seizure of the guards let him do. "I may not be the most accurate Astrologer in the world, but I don't pretend to be— only need to know enough of that dratted craft to cast my own horoscope at the outset of a phase of work, and it helped pick up some extra money here at the palace doing the King's. Maybe some of the news was slanted in a cheery direction, but that doesn't hurt—"

"And why, pray, should an Alchemist, if he's genuine, need to earn any money at all? You *can* turn base metal into gold, can't you? Or can you? If you're the genuine article, as you claim, why haven't you two coins to rub together, old man? Why do you have to steal the King's treasury?"

"Betrayed." King Oliver collapsed onto an empty coffer, wretched with disappointment. "Delver, how could you? Just as we were getting on so well, and I was looking forward to learning about the planets—"

"Sire, I did *not* steal it. Search me, my cellar, you'll find nothing. What would I want it for, anyway? Much too busy to run around spending money; got other things to do."

"I think you'll have quite enough time from now on, Delver. May I suggest, Sire, that Delver be put in one of the small dungeons until he has produced enough gold to prove he is indeed a true Alchemist? Enough being, let us say, the equivalent of what he has stolen from the treasury? If he is an authentic Alchemist, he should have no trouble doing so."

"Capital idea, Bogardus!" But Oliver was still saddened by the defection of someone who had helped relieve the tedium of his kingship. "At least enough to prove he's an Alchemist; replacing the whole treasury sounds a bit much for such an old man, don't you think? Well, that's up to you, Bogardus. See he gets what he needs, equipment, all that, supplies, you know—"

"Take him away, guards. The gray dungeon, I think. I'll have his quarters in town searched, Your Majesty, although I'm sure he's far too clever to have left the gold there."

"Hope it won't take him too long; those planets promised to be quite interesting. Did you have any idea of the tunnel, Bogardus? I do remember some old story of Oliver the Third, I think, having a lady love in town and visiting her by some mysterious passageway."

"Most palaces, Sire, have secret means of entrance and exit for, as you say, lady loves, ambassadors, bankers, moneylenders—people one doesn't particularly want seen entering at the main gates. But as to this one leading through the vault, no; I had always thought it utterly impregnable. After all, this has never happened before in the entire history of the country."

The gates of the gray dungeon had not been kept oiled; they heard a harsh, rusty screech as they slammed shut behind old Delver. The King shivered and kept on toward the stairs leading up to the palace. "I leave it all to you, Bogardus, the whole thing. Get a list from him right away and see that he doesn't dawdle—want my weekly lesson from him if possible." They passed through the padded leather doors that opened to the palace itself.

"Oh, and the worst of it is," Oliver continued as they neared the kitchens, "that I don't suppose now we have enough money to pay for putting raisins in the gruel—"

"And perhaps not for the gruel itself," Bogardus finished.

"There'll be rioting then, mark my words, what with the lake rising and all. Black magic, that's what they'll be saying and you can't tell me not, Bogardus. D'you suppose Delver does have a hand in all that frozen lake business as they say?"

"Undoubtedly, Sire, he is a black magician of the most fell sort. I think we can forestall riots by posting news that he is imprisoned. A firm hand at the helm, and all. Leave it to me, Your Majesty."

"But—but—Bogardus?"

"Sire?"

"Suppose the lake *keeps* rising? Anyway?"

Chapter V

Andrew stood at the foot of the old stone stairs, star-ing about him in horror at the ravaged cellar. Barrels, pots, sacks, boxes, hogsheads, demijohns—the contents were strewn about on the tables and floor; liquids dribbled sadly down the drain in the floor, the ath-anor was smashed, crucibles and retorts and alembics were only shreds of glass mixed with torn books. Even the pathetic feed bags full of straw that had been Andrew's cozy small bed had been ripped open and the contents scattered.

And on top of it all, whoever had done this had torn all the doors off the archways, left them hanging by their hinges. He was too stunned to take the terri-fying but intriguing quick look inside he had always wanted, wondering instead what Mr. Delver would say when he got back? And where was he anyway?

"Andrew!" Sassie came clattering down the stairs, her face as white as pudding for once, her freckles standing out like currants in a bun. "Maam says the palace guards were here and searched the whole cellar for the King's gold and they've arrested

Mr. Delver and put a notice up in front of the palace and he can't get out until he's made enough gold to prove he's a real Alchemist and he's a black magician anyway the notice says and responsible for the pond turning into a lake and rising and oh, Andrew—" she stopped, as aghast as he was at the shambles of the cellar.

"Well, where shall we start?" She seized a broom.

"Did your maam say if the guards *found* any gold?"

"Course not—you know how poor old Mr. Delver is. He does have two brooms, though. Come on, don't just stand there like a stick. Let's get at it."

By nightfall, when Sassie had taken him upstairs to share dinner with her and her mother, they had at least made some progress. The wrecks and ruins of the Alchemist's laboratory had begun to be sorted into piles for re-storing, throwing away as hopeless, mending, and so forth, and Andrew's mattress was re-stuffed. It would be days before it was finished; Andrew wasn't sure he was the right one to do it anyway, but as he swung himself onto his little bed in the cupboard, he thought he might as well try. It would keep him busy and occupied, and even if he did it all wrong and backwards, being busy was something Mr. Delver would approve of.

And so, except for an occasional trip with Sassie in the van to get some light and air, Andrew struggled away in the laboratory, sifting and sorting and labeling and cleaning. By the end of the week he was organized enough to have one entire table covered with objects he didn't know what to do with; other areas—shelves, bins, boxes, and so forth—had been replaced with their contents as intact as Andrew could make them.

The shattered doors to the areas beyond the arches were best left more alone than not, he thought. Since he didn't know what the contents had been before, he couldn't do much about them now and he still had an unexplainable aversion to them. Silly, he thought; this one is just fuel, all kinds—charcoal, straw, hazelwood that pile is, and this is ash bound up in faggots. Nothing sinister about that. Another had great leather bags full of various ores, ingots of lead, and so on; another, just a huge heap of old earth or something. Still, he didn't like any of those spaces, and left them alone as much as he could.

One morning he woke to a bright sunlight coming through the little windows and, getting up, he looked about. The only thing left to do, at long last, was a good scrub-down on the stone floor. By the time the water was boiling and the strong lye soap melted in it, he had breakfasted and, reluctantly, put the ham bone on the fire. He'd made bean soup with it yesterday, after chewing off every morsel of meat and sucking on the gristle. But finally he had to acknowledge that there was no more nourishment in the bone. Only a piece of cheese remained, a small one, and getting a bit ripe smelling, too.

Sassie had helped him when she could, and had told him Mrs. Strawspinner's customers weren't buying from her since her tenant had been locked up for being a black magician. "Tarred with the same brush," Sassie had said, "but Maam says it's an ill wind, you know. She's taking the time to give the kitchen and ovens a good clean, and is painting the cupboards and scrubbing out the stables—busier now than when she had a business!" She had come running down with six new eggs for Andrew—"More than enough for all of us now we don't have any customers to bake for"—and a loaf of bread and pot of butter, so Andrew knew he wouldn't starve.

He set to on the floor with a will, three of the fresh eggs inside him and almost half the loaf, and scrubbed and swashed the hot soapy water into every nook and cranny he could, except under the arches, of course. Without Sassie's telling him he knew the lake had risen during the week, because when he lowered the bucket into the well it took less and less rope than the day before. This morning, though, it seemed the same—yes it was, because he had been keeping knots in the rope to measure. Same level as yesterday.

Grunting under the weight, he put a huge log of ordinary, non-significant everyday oak onto the fire, wiped his hands, and trudged upstairs to spend some time with the Strawspinners while the floor dried. Maybe he could give them a hand with their stable, or something.

But as he whipped out through the little green

door and up the stoop, he noticed the front window was cracked around a hole; a clean rag had been stuffed into it and newspaper pasted with flour paste covered the pane to keep the cold out. "Ah, Andrew, see our medal of honor!" Mrs. Strawspinner came breezing into the front of the shop with a broom and dustpan for the last bits of glass on the floor. "Just received a rock through the window with a note on it—exciting! Like in a story!"

Sassie was in the kitchen, and handed the note to Andrew, staring glumly at the rock on the table. "We knows ye be a witch, old crow," Andrew read. "Git with you and yer brat afore we burn the magician's cellar down."

"Sass, cheer up, girl, our house's solid stone with tile roof; can't burn; you know that. Just as well as y'know Delver's not a black magus or whatever nor I a witch. Ambitious lies, grown up afore their time, that's what that note is. So, Andrew"—and she sat down by him at the table—"saved you a nugget of news from the palace, I did." Mrs. Strawspinner still had her crafty ways, if no customers, and had long ago befriended a little scullery maid in the palace kitchen who would have gone to bed a bit hungry each night, amidst the plenty of the palace, had not Mrs. Strawspinner slipped her a hearty pork, sage, and onion turnover from time to time.

"So I do hear Mr. Delver's just sitting in his cell —the guards were laughing about it—took one piece of dry bread from them one day but otherwise don't eat a thing. Can't say as I blame him; bread and water's not very appetizing, but still—"

"Oh, he never eats anything at all ever—or at least I've never seen him eat. I wonder why he wanted it at all. But they haven't given him any equipment to make the gold, you say?"

"Nary a pot nor jug, the little maid says. He's only got a stool to sit on and a bare floor to sleep on. How they expect the old body to make gold like that's beyond me. More'n some of us think Bogardus wants the man to fail; then he and the King can put the blame on Delver for everything—the bad crops and avalanches and lake and gold disappearing and all —especially now the gruel for the poor an' hapless be running out. Well," she continued, pushing herself up and opening an oven door to check on a pie inside, "wouldn't be the first time a scapegoat got the ax. Speaking of goats, Sass, I'm going to bed right after milking. You can sit up late as you like, but I'm up betimes tomorrow, long afore light. No, don't ask why; maybe I am a witch and, if so, I'm entitled to some secrets. Just you close up the house tight when you do go to bed and bank the fires and all."

That night Andrew finished off the last of the bean and ham-bone soup for his dinner, augmented by the last of the eggs. The heel of the loaf of bread and the last of the smelly cheese would do for breakfast; it was hard to remember that it had only been a few weeks ago he had been sleeping in a coffin, starving and freezing to death and happy at the thought of being devoured by wolves. Now Mr. Delver's seemed almost as much like home as the tinker's wagon had been—except that Pappy had been fun after supper, playing a little violin sometimes, or a tin flute he'd made. It sounded like its own metal, but still, sweet and comfortable and homey.

"Sass! Gosh, I was just getting the blues." Sassie had come down the stairs silently for once, wearing snug little brown felt boots with tassels instead of her usual clattering wooden clogs.

"Yeah, I know. Mé too. I don't like my maam bein' called a witch, even if she is funny-looking." They sat staring into the fire. "Wish I'd thought to bring down some chestnuts to roast. Gee, you really got the place cleaned up just fine, Andrew. It even smells good for a change." She got up and, taking a candle, examined the shelves and tables and cupboards. "Neat as a pin. Hey, what's in this one?" She pulled down a heavy cannister with Delver's violet seal of Hermes's winged cap on top and curious symbols scratched delicately into the metal all around.

"Um, that's—that's Orpiment—No, no, it isn't; it's Ignis Innaturalis. Orpiment's on the other side of the shelf."

"Huh? Ignis what?"

"Innaturalis. Phlogiston to you."

"And what do you call Phlogiston when it's at home?" she demanded, putting the cannister on the table and her hands on her hips.

"Secret fire. Secret because Mr. Delver had to know secrets to make it—I think I'm beginning to understand a little bit of it. Things like coal and Sulphur and soot are full of pure Phlogiston, and Mr.

Delver, Alchemists, get rid of the impure parts and leave the pure Phlogiston behind. I *think* that's sort of how they do gold, too. Mr. Delver was talking under his breath the way he does, you know, and I heard him say something about how as an egg strives to become a chicken, so all metals strive to become gold, and would if they could, only people keep interfering with them and use them for other things."

"Oh. And what are these?" Sassie was looking at more vials and phials.

"Electrum, Quicksilver, Aquaregia, Aqua Fortis, Alkahest—that's the Universal Solvent, that is."

"What?" Sassie looked at him dubiously. "That's silly. If it were a universal solvent what'd you keep it in? Humph. It'd dissolve anything it was in, wouldn't it?"

"I hadn't thought of that." She wandered farther from the table, leaving Andrew realizing how far, how very very far he had to go before he really understood very much of anything, people, or lakes, or alchemy, or anything at all.

Sassie was poking her nose under all the open archways, sniffing and exploring. "Hey, did you ever notice the inside of this crummy old door was painted purple?" she called from the farthest end of the cellar. Andrew got up and went over.

"No, I've never seen it open." He ran his hands over the small shattered door, peering at the inside by lantern light. "Yeah, it is purple." A cold draft came from beyond it; Sassie shivered and they moved back toward the fireplace.

The Adept and Venerable P. C. Delver sat serenely on the small stool his jailer had provided him, meditating philosophically. Which was not easy to do, not for him, since he would infinitely have preferred to be back in his own cellar working on his great Third Step. But being imprisoned, suspected of witchcraft, fraud, and thievery was—to a chosen unfortunate few—as much a part of being an Alchemist as the drudgery of glassblowing, forging, making one's own vessels and tools, doing some things by the light of the moon and others during the day, to say nothing of the nuisance of tending to Frederick twice a year.

Yes, he remembered one of *his* masters when he was a lad telling him of being *years* in a dungeon—they'd been a bit more lavish in that country, though, given old what's-his-name all the equipment and supplies he'd asked for. Still, it'd taken nearly as much argument as art for him to get himself out at long last. There was old L'Achmed, too, who as far as anyone knew was *still* locked up. Just as well, he was always trying to be a legend in his own time and had never been much of an Alchemist anyway. Never even made Adept, as far as Delver knew, and certainly not Venerable.

He thought fleetingly of Andrew, how well the lad had come along, macerating, fixing, crystallizing, filtering; already able to tell a sal from a salt and extract one from another. Quite promising, really.

Delver held the dry piece of bread, what was left of it, in one hand, just to have an object to hold. The guards had taken away even the bundle of horoscopes he'd had, tearing the paper in the process. Pity; as long as Bogardus wasn't doing the King's bidding and letting him have the wherewithal to make that dratted gold, the Prime Minister could have at least let him have the horoscopes to read. All Delver had was a tiny piece of paper that had caught in his crusty old leather coat, a mere corner. How much time had passed since the gate had slammed shut on him? No matter—a week or more—no point trying to keep track.

He'd done what he could with what was at hand, the spiders and the tiny scrap of paper and a pin from his robe and blood from his finger and the bread they insisted on bringing him. That was the best anybody could do—what they could. The rest was up to Andrew. Mr. Delver fell into a sleep that closely resembled hibernation.

"Hey, why didn't you clean out the cobwebs, too?" Sassie asked, plunking herself down on a stool by the fire.

"Well, Mr. Delver seems to like them. They were here when I got here and—say, there's a spider on your sleeve; hold still and I'll get it off. That's funny, they usually stay way up there."

Sassie held very still while Andrew gently brushed the spider onto his hand off her sleeve. She looked down at it curiously.

"I've never seen a blue spider with light brown legs before. What kind is it?"

Andrew spread out his hand by the lantern light. "It isn't blue; it's wrapped up in a scrap of paper, blue paper, with its brown legs sticking out. Sassie, you must have gotten that on your sleeve when we were over by the purple door. All Delver's spiders up there on the ceiling are black as can be and this *is* light brown. Here, you hold its front legs and I'll get the paper off."

The spider, shed of its wrapping and quite exhausted, reeled straight for the heel of bread on the table to refresh itself while Andrew and Sassie peered at the tiny bit of paper. So tiny it could barely hold the letters that looked às if they had been scratched on with a pin dipped in—blood? Andrew recognized the paper as being from Delver's roll of horoscopes. He automatically reached for the bronze mirror and read

A: USE YOUR WITS! P.C.D. <u>Adpt</u>. Ven.
Those twenty-two tiny letters had taken up both sides of the paper.

"Why's Adpt. underlined, Andrew?"

"Wait a minute—let me think. It must be—oh, golly." Andrew buried his head in his hands, his blood racing fast, trying to remember. Sassie very sensibly left him alone, and took the lantern back to the purple door and peered as far into the gloom beyond it as she could. It seemed to go on and on, and there was definitely a very cold draft coming through.

"Sass! I've got it! The day he explained 'Adept' to me and gave me my pointed hat!" Andrew

quickly explained about the hat going to the Apprentice of an Adept, and the Adept changing his name, and all that, and then, "D'you see? He *has* made gold already or he *couldn't* call himself Adept, and it's somewhere here. He swore he didn't need it once he'd made it, and never thought of spending it or the rules didn't permit it or something. The gold he's made has got to be here somewhere!"

"But, Andrew, wouldn't the guards have found it? Lordy, they sure tore the place apart looking for it. And if *they* didn't, wouldn't *you* have, putting the place back together again?"

They sat in the firelight, stumped, Andrew picking at a hangnail he'd gotten from the strong lye soap and water he'd used on the floor.

"Don't pick," Sassie scolded.

"Don't pick on me—Sass! The other-colored stones! Come here!" He'd noticed them again this morning when he was scrubbing down the floor, the patch of lighter-colored stones washing almost white from the mud and ashes the guards had ground into the whole floor.

Sassie looked up at him, glowing, running her square brown hands over the stones. "Get a pick, a shovel!"

"No, a chisel first, you dope—"

Half an hour later, if they had bothered to look at an hourglass, which they hadn't, they were heaving and struggling with a leather sling they had managed to slip under a chamois-wrapped bundle in the bottom of the hole they had dug. Getting the stones out had been the most difficult; they were as tightly fitted together as mortal enemies and Andrew had had to grind the chisel down to hairbreadth fineness to get it in at all, Sassie gamefully sweating at turning the enormous grindstone. But the ground underneath was sandy, soft; it was the sheer weight of the bundle that was making the sweat break out on their upper lips and foreheads now. Slowly it came up, and they eased it out onto a level stone in the floor. Wrapped in chamois, bound with a fine strong cord, and, like everything else in Delver's stores, sealed with the sign of Hermes.

"Come on, Andrew, just because you're his Apprentice doesn't mean you can't make a decision once in a while. If I waited for Maam to tell me every time when to take things out of the oven or put them in—"

"Okay, OKAY!" Andrew slashed the cord apart with the chisel; the moldering chamois skin fell away in decaying folds.

Gold. Chunks, nuggets, ingots, lumps. The purest gold, some coolly whitish, some with a redder hue, but gold, undeniably, gold! The gold of an Adept. The gold of Mr. P. C. Delver.

"Sure that's not too heavy?" Andrew looked worriedly at Sassie, who had taken half the gold and made a strong leather backpack for each of them out of an old robe of Delver's. They were tied on now with stout rope to help support the weight; Andrew was looking dubiously at the scant level of oil in the lantern, knowing the oilcan was empty.

"Nope." Sassie was stuffing the rest of the bread and cheese Andrew had set aside for his breakfast into the buttoned pocket of her sturdy wool petticoat. "After all, we don't know how long this is going to take. Wish I'd brought some hard-boiled eggs. Well, no time for that. This'll have to do for rations."

Well, Andrew thought, not enough oil and in that draft a candle would never do. He put on his pointed hat to give him authority, and, seizing the cannister of Ignis Innaturalis, broke the seal. Not knowing what to expect, he lifted the lid off the cannister, shielding his eyes.

Nothing. He looked in; it seemed to be full of—oil? Perhaps it needed a wick, to be lit. Pouring a bit of the liquid into a saucer, he reached for a wick in the table drawer, thinking to experiment with just a small amount at first, but as soon as the cannister was half-emptied of the liquid a powerful glow emerged from the substance left inside. Blue, cold, piercing, it illuminated the entire cellar from one end to another.

"Wow!" Sassie crowed. "I don't care what you call it, it's just what we need! Let's go!"

Andrew was still full of ifs. "The passage might end in a wall, or get too small, or—"

"Or, or, or—Andrew, d'you think Mr. Delver'd have sent that spider if he thought there wasn't a way for you to get to him? No wonder he said USE

YOUR WITS! Come on, use 'em. He meant for you to bring him the gold—that's why he underlined Adpt. —so he can get out of the dungeon. He just doesn't know how lucky he is I'm here to explain it all." And Sassie charged straight into the passageway, letting Andrew hold up the cannister of Phlogiston above their heads as they left the ruined purple door far behind.

But Andrew had been right; the passageway rapidly turned into a narrowing and lowering tunnel rather soon; still, not too low nor too narrow. He could imagine Delver having to stoop considerably, but it was a passage. The light of the secret fire showed distinct pools of water as they wound their way down, down. Perhaps, he thought, the rising lake was seeping in here; they were surely below the level of the town now and must have passed under the palace wall.

"Shush—you hear anything?" Sassie turned her head back, listening. Andrew heard his own heart pounding, but he expected that.

"What sort of thing?"

"A sort of—scraping, I guess—metallic." Sassie was listening intently; Andrew thought he did hear not only a scraping but something rather like a rusty stiff bellows. Echoes from the stone walls made it hard to tell how far behind or exactly where it was coming from, but surely they would have seen anything, the light he was carrying was so bright, if it were very near.

Before he could ask Sassie what she thought—
and she was certainly thinking something, her square
little brown face screwed up so she looked more like
her mother than usual—there was a tremendous rum-
ble, a sudden airlessness, and then the world crashed
in behind them. Rocks and debris and mortar came
crashing down, crashing the cannister of secret fire
from Andrew's hand into the pool of water Sassie
was lying in, extinguishing the fire, and above all,
knocking Andrew completely unconscious.

Sassie sat quite still; she had pulled Andrew from
the fallen rocks and got herself out of the pool of icy
water. Somehow or other, with the weight of both
their shares of gold to add to the effort, she had managed to get Andrew's head in her lap and her back
propped up against a boulder. She couldn't see what
it was, but it must have been a boulder; it was ridgy
and uncomfortable. The wet spot on Andrew's forehead was likely blood, she thought; it was thick,
warm, and sticky—but there didn't seem to be too
much of it, or she hoped not.

The next thing to do was to retrieve the cannister of secret fire from the puddle of water that
had extinguished it, but something—some memory,
something—held Sassie back for a moment. And then
there was a scrabbling, tearing, clunking of rock
very, very near, as if something were trying to get
through the rockfall that blocked their return to the
cellar. The noise came near, and nearer, and she

heard the splat of something in the pool of ice water, and a more slithery sound, and smelled something stale, fetid, and sour slithering over her small soggy felt boots with their little brown tassels. Sassie sat still, half her mind trying to recall what it was that seemed so terribly important to remember right now, and the other half resolved not to scream no matter what. She had her hands over Andrew's face, protecting what she could of him from the huge, stinking, slithering horror that seemed to be surrounding them both.

She felt a tearing at her long brown pigtail, then a snuffling at her sleeve, and finally a great ripping at her skirt.

And the snuffling stopped, and the slither retreated, the clanking and wheezing withdrawing through shattered rock, until the air was clear to her smell again and the sound had totally vanished.

Shifting Andrew from her lap as gently as possible, she fumbled around on her hands and knees in the pool at the bottom of the tunnel, finally finding the cannister at last. As she lifted it out of the water and drained it, the blessed blue flame burst up again, as strong as ever.

Andrew muttered weakly, his eyelids flickered. She found a handkerchief and mopped his face with the ice water from the pool; the cut on his forehead was small, as she'd thought. Trying to remember what her maam had told her to do for blows on the head, all she could remember was "feed a cold and starve a fever"—or was it the other way around?

Being her mother's daughter, she decided in any situation a little something to eat couldn't hurt. She fumbled in her pocket for the bread and cheese.

It was gone. Every last crumb. So that was what the horrible thing had slit her skirt for!

"Sass?" Andrew was coming round now, trying to sit up. Least said the better, she thought.

"You okay, Andrew? There was sort of a rock-slide; you got knocked out." The thing to do was get the job done, and Andrew was pale enough already without her sharing her fright during the time he'd been unconscious. Whatever it had been had gone, leaving a hole large enough for them to crawl through if they wanted to go back. Sassie didn't, not only because of Mr. Delver being somewhere in front of them and not behind, but because she didn't cotton to trailing quite so close on the path of the "slither," and if Andrew knew about it she was sure he wouldn't either. But he had enough on his shoulders, quite literally, with the heavy pack of gold, and his old head probably aching like fury.

"Yeah, I'm okay now. Just a minute, I'll get up." She gave him her shoulder and he pulled himself up; they readjusted the heavy packs of gold, and Andrew straightened the brim of his pointed hat.

But no sooner had they gone ahead some ten paces, when the tunnel branched in two, with a fork leading off to the right, sloping down distinctly, where the fork to the left began a gentle rise. They stopped, looking for some sign, some indication of which turn to take.

"There's more cold draft coming from the right-hand one," Andrew noted, peering down as far as he could, "and I'd think we'd have gotten close enough to the palace by now so things would start getting warmer as well as higher, don't you?"

"Hey, yeah, I do. Okay, the left-hand one." Sassie plunged on ahead, and in another few paces they found they were still going up, but the tunnel had become less a tunnel than a broad, low, stone corridor. "Andrew, it's almost civilization!" she hissed.

And for a moment they were almost glad to see the heavy wooden wall that blocked their further passage, so clearly a part of the palace. The left fork had been the right choice after all. But the secret fire showed no door, nor knob.

"What d'you think?" Sassie asked, running her hand over it as high and wide as she could.

"Well,"—Andrew's wits were all back now—"if the spider got through with Delver's message—" He pushed at the wall, shoved, hoping to find a secret catch. "Hey, come hold the light for me!" A grubby tuft of old gray fur was caught in one of the closely joined boards. Mr. Delver's puce leather coat, the lining! "He's been here!" Andrew crowed. "We're on the right track!"

At last Andrew found what he was looking for: hair-thin hinges joining two planks, and just below the tuft of fur, a tiny keyhole.

Drumming through Andrew's head, which was still throbbing a bit, were the words on Delver's tiny message: USE YOUR WITS. So far they had, and done pretty well, too. Had Delver foreseen this? He must have.

"Sassie, d'you have a pin or a piece of wire or something like that on you?"

She was quick with a disappointed "Nope, I don't. . . ." Andrew was thinking with his fingertips now; suddenly he pulled off his pointed hat. Of course! The wires that stiffened the point! He quickly pulled one of the ribs out, put his hat back on for good luck, and bent over the lock.

"Jeepers!" Sassie whispered. "Where'd you learn to do that?"

"Pappy, of course. How can you repair locks and all that without knowing how they work? Hush up now, it's coming—and we don't know what's on the other side."

The door opened slowly, heavily, into gloom and shadows; yet one more cold chamber, but the air at their backs from the tunnel was far colder. Andrew capped the cannister of secret fire quickly; there was a dim glow farther ahead. They stood in the arched room, looking at the empty shelves, coffers, bins.

"Sass, it's the royal treasury!" The dim light from the passage outside the open wrought-iron grills showed the sad remains, the crown jewels in their glass case. Andrew felt suddenly sorry for King Oliver that the thief had spurned Oliver's regalia, yet taken everything else. They tiptoed to the iron gates, hugging the shadows.

P. C. Delver dozed a bit, memories of his early boyhood in a faraway land stretching to his farewell to his family as a lad, the great Celsus having apprenticed him for the sum of fifty retas. They had journeyed across water; Delver as a lad alternating between seasickness and homesickness but still with a wild, irrepressible certainty that he was in for great things. . . .

Great things. Decades of work, how many he no longer knew or cared. Hard work; staying up at night; little food—so little he had long ago stopped needing it at all; small sleep; seclusion, seclusion, no one understood that necessity. Even the endless, interminable correspondence with other Alchemists in faraway lands was unnourishing these days—there was nothing except the known, the commonplace, to write to each other in their ancient codes and cyphers; and they all lied to each other like fury anyway, like old women exchanging recipes for a cake and leaving out the one indispensable ingredient. Somehow he thought Mrs. Strawspinner would understand that, and disapprove quite strongly. Perhaps not, perhaps she was a bit of an Alchemist in her own way—Alchemy and cooking were, when you came down to it, much alike; reorganization of materials. And where some were better at their art than others, there was no explanation.

Delver jolted upright on his stool; the signal he had been waiting for had come. A small one, almost imperceptible, but from the hall leading to the treasure vault he had felt a puff, a merest whiff of damp clammy cold air, heard the merest scurry of something.

"Guard! GUARD!" he boomed, rattling his belt buckle on the bars of the cell.

"What is it now, old fool?" The guard who came was knuckling sleep from gummy eyes.

"What do you mean, now? Haven't said a word to you since they shut me up in here."

"Well, must have been dreaming of another prisoner somewhere else. Been in the dungeon racket too long. What'cha want?"

"Not what I want, what *they* want. You may now tell that Prime Minister Bogardus that the gold for my ransom is ready."

"Where? What?" The guard rubbed his eyes again, peering into the gloom of the gray dungeon.

"Aha, not for your eyes, my good man, for his. Run along now and fetch him." The guard waddled as fast as he could up the stone hallway, past the leather doors that let in a whiff of the palace kitchens and disappeared.

"Andrew!" hissed Delver as loud as he dared, poking his hand as far out of the bars as he could. "ANDREW! This way!"

Pushing open the gates from the treasury, Andrew and Sassie broke into a clumsy trot at the sound of Delver's voice. There he was, his great nose sticking out between iron bars!

"Oh, Mr. Delver! Here!" They quickly shed their leather packs and shoved the bits and coins and bars of gold as fast as possible, piece by heavy piece, between the bars of his cell.

74

"Hurry, lad, hurry. See you used your wits and brought a cohort. Just as well, had forgotten there was *this* much gold. Vulgar, really—but I need it all." He was stacking the nuggets, chunks, bars, and lumps in the middle of his cell. "Where was it, by the way? I had forgotten. Knew you could find it if you used your noodle; the thing that took me the longest was training that dratted spider. Independent cuss, but I see he finally got to you."

"Yes, tonight. The gold was under some stones by the arches—a different color stone—" They were puffing and panting, all three. Suddenly a distinct smell of burning cherry tarts came down the corridor; the leather doors must have opened. "Quick," hissed Delver, "back where you came from. Here comes Bogardus!"

It was Sassie who was almost seen; she remembered to scoop up the telltale leather and rope of their empty packs before squeezing into the darkest corner of the treasury with Andrew. They could hear, over the pounding of their hearts, the velvet and sable and silk susurrus of Bogardus' robes as the Prime Minister came down the passage and stopped in front of Delver's cell, unlocking it with a great key.

"So, you say you've produced your ransom, hmm, Delver?" The haughty voice of the Prime Minister carried over the squeaking of the dungeon door being opened.

"As you required, Bogardus. As you required. And with no help from you, as you promised and as

King Oliver directed, I might add." Delver sounded more than a little proud of himself; Sassie could see a faint grin on Andrew's face in the dim light that reached them.

"So I see—very clever, very clever indeed." And suddenly Bogardus was coming toward the treasury itself; Sassie pulled Andrew down behind a great empty bin and would have stopped their breathing if she could have. Bogardus strode in fearlessly, seized the handle of an empty chest, and dragged it back down the passage and into Delver's cell.

"Put the gold in there, old fool—quickly!" They could hear Delver grunt and gasp as he lifted piece after piece of the heavy rich metal and placed it gently in the chest; then the lid of the chest slamming shut. A moment later, the chest was in the passage outside the cell and the door had slammed shut, the key screeching in the lock.

"But—but you must let me go now. I've done as you required; what more do you want? Heaps of gold, you said, and there it is, in that chest right in front of you. You *must* let me out now. I've proved I'm a genuine Alchemist and made gold from base metal. Those were your *terms!*" Andrew found it somehow quite dreadful to hear the usually imperious Delver pleading, begging.

"Were they?" They could imagine Bogardus stroking his satiny black goatee. "It really doesn't matter. No one knows of the gold, the guard didn't see it, and by the time the King comes down to see how you're doing—he's very forgetful, you know, and I shan't remind him—your gold too will have disappeared. Your word against mine, won't it be? I rather think our dimwitted King will believe me before you, Delver, I truly do. Your problem, it seems to me, is whether to make another batch, if you can. hoping for a second time to obtain your freedom. Or whether to simply languish away here. I really can't advise you, for I'm a liar at best and utterly untrustworthy."

Bogardus dragged the gold-laden chest through the treasury and into the tunnel Andrew and Sassie had come through, leaving it on the far side of the secret door in the shelves. Even he was puffing a bit as he went back through and past Delver's cell.

"Good night, Delver. I leave you to your meditations." They heard the rustle of his robes on the floor as the Prime Minister returned to the palace.

"Sass, I'm sorry, but *that* lock on Delver's cell is just too much for me—" They were well inside the tunnel now, heading back for the cellar. When they had dared return to Delver's cell for advice, or instructions, they had found him, quite surprisingly, sound asleep on the small three-legged stool, as if he weren't troubled at all.

"Okay, it sure looked like a stinker—but oh, that Bogardus! He's really *wicked*, Andrew."

"And the worst of it is that we can't even say anything about it—I mean, Delver *did* make the gold, but not—not—"

"Not the way they expected. Or maybe the *way* they expected, but not *when*. Myself, I don't see it matters if the darn stuff was made fifty years ago or yesterday, gold's gold. Oh, I'd love to put that Bogardus in Maam's oven for three weeks!"

Sassie was so angry she had forgotten about whatever it was that such a short time before had slithered and scraped and slathered over them in the total dark; her wits were, however, sharp enough to have her think of their taking just one small piece each of Delver's gold from the chest Bogardus had hidden in the tunnel. It was clearly Delver's, every piece had been marked with his seal of the winged hat of Hermes, although what they would do with it they scarcely knew.

"Andrew! Let's take the right fork and see where it goes!" They had reached the branching of the tunnel; Sassie's feet in their square little felt boots were soaked and Andrew's head still ached badly, but they were too angry to give up and just return home.

Only the secret fire, the Ignis Innaturalis, seemed not to have failed them; Andrew held it up as they took the unexplored fork of the tunnel and started down, down, pushing against the icy air that rose. The tunnel stopped abruptly at an iron ladder that descended into a round hole; even the secret fire could not show them the bottom.

"Me first," Sassie said, and started down the ladder after helping Andrew lash the cannister of light to his arm to free his hands for climbing. Down and down, it seemed endless, and colder and colder.

Until another light began to show, and the ladder ended. They were in a true cave, a natural pocket in the mountainside. "Andrew, this must be in the cliff face the palace is built on!" Sassie whispered. The frozen opal of dawn was just showing through a clay-and-wattle screen that shut off the cave's opening; ice had built up on it outside so it must be invisible from the lake, Andrew thought, not that anybody's out on the lake. He poked a small hole through one of the chinks; yes, the lake was there, directly outside.

Sassie had already crawled up on the enormous, heavy sledge that almost filled the cave, except for an enclosure that held four great cart horses, whuffling and stomping in their stalls. Andrew climbed up beside her; whatever was on the sledge was covered with thick tarred cloth and well tied down, except for one chest at the end which left only room enough for one more box before the sledge was fully loaded.

"Andrew!" Sassie was peering into the box; she had pried up a slat of wood just enough to see inside. "It's the King's treasury! Look!"

She drew out a handful of coins—gold coins with the King's profile, silver coins with the crown— gems and pearls and gold, gold, gold. Andrew touched a deep green stone with the tip of his finger; it must be an emerald, he thought.

"Sssst! Quick, hide!" There was only time for them to put a coin and jewel or two in their pockets before Sassie pulled him over the far side of the sledge and under it; the chest Bogardus had filled with Mr. Delver's gold was slowly descending in front of the ladder, lashed with rope and swaying slowly. It came to rest with a rich thunk on the cave's floor, the long rope tumbling after it and followed by the unmistakable boots and robes of the Prime Minister, virtually tumbling down the ladder in haste. Bogardus heaved the chest onto the sledge, lashed it down, and covered it with the last of the tarred cloth. He hastily watered the horses and strewed a stingy handful of oats in their mangers before repeating Andrew's action of poking a hole through the icy wattle screen and staring out at the lake. He turned back, smiling and rubbing his hands in delight; patted the side of the sledge and quickly climbed up the ladder and out of sight. Underneath the sledge, Andrew watched the last of Bogardus rising up the ladder; he turned and saw that Sassie, on the other hand, was turned the other way.

"We'd better give him a good chunk of time to get back to the palace before we climb up to the tunnels ourselves," Andrew cautioned her.

"Yep, but not *too* long. I have the feeling he'll be back down here before long." She pointed significantly at the tiny tongue of water that was edging underneath the clay-and-wattle screen at the entrance to the cave.

Andrew nodded in comprehension. A few moments later, the Phlogiston capped for safety, they climbed up the ladder and turned to the dark tunnel leading to Mr. Delver's cellar.

"And the thing is, Maam, that if old Bogardus doesn't get the sledge out with the treasure he's stolen —the whole country's treasure, not just Mr. Delver's gold—now, or pretty soon, he won't be able to at all. The cave'll flood if the lake does keep rising, and if it goes down the sledge won't go over the old stone fields. He must have been waiting for just this kind of ice, that comes right up to the edge."

They had been sitting in Mrs. Strawspinner's kitchen, their stomachs full of hot porridge and honey, cocoa and cream, their damp clothes steaming from the heat of the oven, when she had come in from her early morning jaunt. Skates were dangling from their laces over her shoulder, and for the first time Andrew had seen her wrinkled nutlike face rosier than it was brown, a sparkle of excitement in it even as she measured the dank tatters of their clothes and the bruise and cut on Andrew's head and the sodden mess of Sassie's tasseled boots.

Now, hearing their tale, she poured herself another cup of coffee and sat beside them in the kitchen, the canary chirping a song as unlikely a counterpoint to their story as anything could be. She rubbed her nose, she rubbed her forehead, she cracked her knuckles and drank some coffee. Finally she spoke.

"Sass, you and Andrew get into whatever good dry clothes you have, warmish like too, and wash your faces and so on while I get Raisin hitched up to the van. We're going to pay a call. On the King."

Chapter VI

It took Mrs. Strawspinner less time to get in to see King Oliver than was known in history. The three modest townspeople, two of them children, had scarcely sat down in the palace anteroom, after Mrs. Strawspinner had handed a small, sealed parcel to the chamberlain, than the latter had reopened the door to the King's presence and beckoned them in, far ahead of their turn and leaving several ministers, bankers, and court functionaries cooling their heels on the marble floors.

King Oliver was sitting on the state throne, well wrapped up in ermine velvet and his feet on a brocade footstool; he was licking his fingers as they came in and Andrew and Sassie could see crumbs of chocolate cake on the lace handkerchief he had spread over his lap.

"Madam!" Delight filled his face as Mrs. Strawspinner did the best she could with a curtsy, which wasn't much except to have a knee pop loudly and her old waxed felt cloak crackle like cold taffy. Sassie bobbed up and down like a jack-in-the-box; Andrew bowed, holding his pointed hat in front and wishing he had a feather in it or something to make it a bit more graceful; he wasn't accustomed to bowing.

"Madam Strawspinner! Welcome, welcome, welcome!"

"Mrs. Strawspinner will do very nicely, Your Majesty. I hope you enjoyed the little sweetmeat I sent in, Sire?"

"The aroma! The texture!" King Oliver waved his everyday second-best scepter in a circle. "Incredible! Poetry! Magic! You haven't brought another, by any chance, have you?"

"Not this morning, Your Majesty, but I'll be delighted to send you a dozen every week, at a very reasonable price, of course, as soon as our business with you is finished."

"Only a dozen a week? Will that be enough, d'you think?"

"Oh yes, since they'll be packed in with some other little goodies, variations on recipes I've been perfecting recently. Chocolate gumballs, for instance, a particular kind of almond tart, that sort of thing."

"Ah, almonds, yes—" King Oliver closed his eyes in a reverie.

"I say, Your Majesty, is there a spare chair or so around? The three of us have had quite a night." Mrs. Strawspinner drew him back to reality. He clapped his pudgy little hands; chairs were brought, and Mrs. Strawspinner began her tale. Once his mind was off the subject of food, King Oliver found he was actually enjoying a morning's real work. Heaven knew where Bogardus was—hadn't shown up for the first time in years.

"So you see, Sire," Mrs. Strawspinner concluded the tale of Andrew's and Sassie's discoveries, "the royal treasure is all packed up in chests and boxes tied onto a sledge in a cave right under your palace, and Bogardus has just been waiting for the lake to rise to the right level to make his escape. Nothing to do with Mr. Delver at all, except that at the last minute he stole Mr. Delver's gold too. Show the King, Andrew."

Poor King Oliver was slightly uncomfortable; if Bogardus had betrayed him was he, Oliver the Eleventh, equal to the job of ruling his own kingdom? Oh, dear—but here was the young Apprentice holding out a handful of gold coins, unmistakably his own, an emerald and pearl or two, and the little brown girl had a strange lump of gold with a curious seal on it in her small fist. Oh dear, oh dear. Nothing for it, he must take charge.

"Guard! Release Mr. Delver from the gray dungeon at once! Full apologies, all that sort of thing. Delighted to see him here at his convenience; all restitution and all that sort of thing. . . ." Oliver leaned back, relieved. After all, that hadn't been so hard and it was *his* kingdom, not Bogardus'.

"Now that's right on the button, Sire," Mrs. Strawspinner said, "and I don't doubt Mr. Delver'll be pleased to be his own man again. Now for the good news—Sass, you and Andrew listen close too. Now you all know about the ugly feeling in the town about Mr. Delver, and how it spilled over so's nobody'd buy their baked goods from me these last days either—and then there were the poor farmers from the mountains whose crops failed because of last summer's rain and hail, and were reduced to your gruel, Sire—well, in any event empty stomachs of any sort never contribute to sound thinking."

"Quite right, Madam, quite, quite right."

"In any event, Sire, lack of business gave me some time to myself for a change, and after I'd done all my odd jobs around the house and stables, I suddenly bethought me that last night was winter solstice. Now when I was a young girl 'twas always the custom to stay up from midnight till noon, all the young folk, for solstice be when the sun stands at its lowest, then starts moving back up toward summer. Oh, we'd have bonfires, you know, and skate on the little pond, and roast a pig, and so on. Young folk don't do that any more, so far as I know, but it was fun. Well, silly of me I know, old widdy lady like I am, but I felt like a good long skate on that there lake out there last night—pond never was very big and froze rough, too. Well, couldn't resist, so I put myself to bed early and got up—not at midnight, too old for that, but about four by church bells—and off I went. Oh, it was beautiful, Sire, the last of the moon kept me going till first light, when the mountaintops look like beaten egg white, you know—"

"Mercy me, Mrs. S.," the King interrupted, "you mean you skated all the way to the far side of the lake? Till dawn? Weren't you afraid?" The

King's mouth hung open in awe. "It's evil, that lake. We all know that."

" 'Tis not. Only think that because old Bogardus told everyone so to keep their minds off his making off with the gold. No more evil than daybreak, which is when I got to the far side and found where the lake is coming from! That last big avalanche, the one that carried away Andrew's pappy, took all the trees and grass and earth down with it. A big piece of that mountainside's gone and coming out of it is the most beautiful river you've ever seen—must have been pent up underground all these years. Well, it's not any more. It's filling the old stone and thistle fields and making a real lake we can use! Boating, fishing, skating in the winter!"

"But, Madam, we'll all be drowned if it keeps on rising and the river keeps on pouring out!"

"Ah, but it won't. 'Cause after I found the source of the lake I skated on around the edge of the whole thing, widdershins like—and lucky I was to have chosen that way 'stead of clockwise, I can tell you, because I was present at the birth of a water-fall!"

"Maam!" Sassie gasped.

"Yes'm, and yes, Your Majesty. There I was, with the wind at my back, holding out my old cloak here and just almost sailing along, so little effort with the ice so smooth and all. Then that awful sound behind me, just at the gap that we used to have to use to get to the lowland marsh before you put in that eastern road for us. Well, 'twas a terrible ava-

87

lanche coming down, fearful and had I been going t'other way, as I say, I'da been taken with it. But when all the snow and ice and glacier had settled, it'd cracked open and taken with it enough of the old gap so the extra water from the lake stopped being pent up in our valley and began pouring down and down into the marsh. Now I expect your engineers and all can tell you 'bout how much lake we're likely to have left once things settle down, but I should think—and you need to be a good judge of how much batter a baking pan'll hold in my trade—we'll have still a good-size lake up here come summer, and on top of it all, King Oliver Falls!"

"King Oliver Falls!" the little monarch whispered, his thoughts full of travelers coming from afar to see the wonder, and a royal barge of his very own to use on the lake for picnics and such, and fireworks reflected in the water on his birthday. "King Oliver Lake, King Oliver Falls. Then the level of the water should begin to go down now a bit?"

"Yes indeed, which is why we're here in the first place. Bogardus is bound to notice and make his escape with the treasures now, while he can get the sledge out of the cave and across the lake to the high road, Your Majesty. And only you can stop him."

Prime Minister Bogardus had finished hitching the vast horses to the sledge; they were frisky and hungry and eager for exercise; it would be a job controlling them in the beginning. The cargo on the sledge was securely tied down; Bogardus seized a crowbar and began hacking at the icy screen that had covered the cave's opening for so many weeks. Perfect; the ice came just to the edge. He leaped up on the seat, seized the reins in velvet-gloved hands, and cracked the whip. The horses charged forth into the bright day, their cleated shoes crunching firmly into the ice.

Only to find, as he turned on the curve past the thicket of evergreens lining the shore, the entire palace guard, led by King Oliver himself on a white stallion, barring his way and the King grinning triumphantly. Next to the royal stallion was the tiny little van of that hag, Strawspinner, with her brat and Delver's Apprentice on the seat beside her, laughing and cheering.

Only one thing to do; Bogardus flailed the horses with his whip hard enough to bring blood, and as he jumped off and ran back into the cave, the great sledge with its powerful team tangled and crashed into the guard, scattering them for long enough for Bogardus to be well up the ladder and into the tunnel leading to Delver's cellar. Far better to try to escape through town than through the palace; it would take the guard just long enough to reassemble themselves and catch the runaway sledge for Bogardus to make good his escape.

And surely that old fool Delver would have something of value in his cellar he could take with him? A bit of leftover gold, perhaps, if nothing else. Bogardus' own purse was full, his garments richly

embroidered in bullion, pearls, rare jewels, and even the tassels and braid on his boots were of thick gold thread; he could live for quite a time and very well too on just the value of what he had on his back. But to him, enough was *not* as good as a feast. Bursting out of the tunnel, he began ransacking the shelves, cupboards, and drawers of the old Alchemist's cellar, oblivious to a dark shadow upright in a distant corner.

Nothing, not so much as a silver button or shoe buckle! Furious, Bogardus' eye lit on the shattered doors under the arches, dimly visible in the sunshine coming in the little windows high above. Dashing into one, he saw a heap of dry, earthy substance with a fearful stink to it and was on the point of searching the next arch when he spied a shovel, small, delicately wrought, with runes and symbols engraved on the handle, stuck in the pile. Hmmm—something important here! Only a few scoops with the shovel, and the sound of metal on—metal! With frantic haste he scooped again; the top of a large vessel—gold, could it be gold?—appeared. Faster and faster; the vessel as it was uncovered resembled more and more an enormous brazen turnip with a copper lid, almost as large as Bogardus himself. Beautifully wrought, not gold after all but surely *containing* gold! Clever of Delver to have buried it under a dungheap, no wonder his guards hadn't found it when they had searched before. He tossed aside the shovel, found the clasp and threw back the cover with one hand, opening his purse to fill it with more gold, the gold he knew was inside.

P. C. Delver, Adept and Venerable, stood invisibly in the shadows of his cellar watching Bogardus in his frantic search for one last piece of gold. Delver had hurried from that dreary gray dungeon straightaway back to his beloved cellar, so eager was he to get back to work. A whole week, more very likely—couldn't keep track—lost on the great Third Step! And decades more to go! He almost gnashed his teeth in frustration, but he sensed the inconveniences and interruptions of recent events were not yet quite over; that there was a thing or two he might have to cope with before his life was his own again.

Yes, footsteps in the tunnel, running. Delver placed the small shovel he had so carefully made under the sign of the planet Jupiter so many years ago so it would catch a ray of sunlight, took to the shadows himself, and waited. Bogardus, all right, as he knew it would be. The man's greed was insatiable. Well, Frederick would take care of him in short order. *Then* Delver could get back to work. All that beautiful glass to blow all over again . . .

There was a horrible, unearthly scream from Bogardus, cut short as if with a sharp knife. The clatter of horses' hoofs sounded in the street above, the wheels of Mrs. Strawspinner's little van. Guards clattered down the stone stairs, Andrew and Sassie among them, then Mrs. Strawspinner herself, followed by the King, puffing and panting. For once Mr. Delver was prepared to accept the intrusion. He sighed, and from somewhere inside summoned up a smile, untucking his hands from the sleeves of his grubby puce-colored robe, and stepped forward to greet them.

They found Mr. Delver under one of the arches, carefully looking at the ceiling with his hands behind his back, as he deftly closed the lid of a huge, glittering brass vessel and locked the silver clasp with a key of pure crystal. He came forward with a rusty smile on his face, leaving behind him not only the vessel but an incredibly lifelike marble statue of a man frozen in a state of horror, one hand reaching out avidly and the other opening a purse, already stuffed with stone coins.

"I say, Delver," the King called, "that statue's a dead ringer for Bogardus! Seen him anywhere? Got away from us through the tunnel; left the treasure with us though. We've got the palace surrounded but thought he might try to get away through here—clever fellow."

"Yes, I've seen your Bogardus, Your Majesty, and so has Frederick. That *is* Bogardus—" and Delver pointed over his shoulder to the marble statue. "Be obliged if you'd take him away as soon as possible, too. Haven't room to store him for you and, even if I did, I need Andrew to help me get back to work instead of dusting off statues."

Andrew and Sassie stood in front of the King

and Mrs. Strawspinner, looking at the incredible ice-cold stone that had been Prime Minister Bogardus. Even Mrs. Strawspinner was in awe. "Better than I could carve out of butter any day, Mr. Delver. How'd you do it?"

"Me?" Delver was already seizing the bellows and building up the fire. "Didn't do it at all. Chap's own greed brought him to it. Uncovered that vessel under the dungheap where Frederick lives and like a dratted fool he opened it." Turning back to the fire, Delver thought it was none of their business that he'd deliberately left the shovel out, and the vessel unlocked. Tee hee, he thought.

"Ugh," Sassie said, "that whole part of the cellar smells like what was in the tunnel last night—"

"In the tunnel? With *you?*" Delver dropped the bellows in distress.

"Yep." And Sassie went on to explain about the slithering horror; she showed them the slit in her skirt and her torn pocket in her petticoat. Andrew was already pale and Delver wasn't looking quite as chipper as he had a moment ago. And Sassie found as she finished she was holding one of her mother's hands.

"What day was yesterday? Ah, yes, winter solstice!" Delver laid his thumb on his chin. "The old devil—I forgot I'd left his vessel unlocked. Intended to feed him after Andrew went to bed that night but got locked up myself instead. Frederick gets fed twice a year, all he needs, winter and summer solstices. He must have smelled your bread and cheese, young lady, and followed you through the tunnel to get his feed. That's the trouble with Basilisks, clumsy, all thumbs and claws and scales and knobs, shattering rocks with their bodies—well, lucky for you the Ignis Innaturalis was out and not lighting up the place, or you'd be in the same state as Bogardus here."

"My God! A BASILISK!" King Oliver was white with fear.

"Of course a Basilisk. Bogardus and Frederick got a good clear look at each other and as night follows day, Bogardus turned to solid stone!"

"Well, I'm certainly not going to have that creature in my house one more minute, I can tell you that!" Mrs. Strawspinner was sputtering. "There's a clause in our lease somewhere, Mr. Delver, that says something about things like that."

"Andrew, get the shovel and cover him up again; he'll sleep till summer now he's had his feed. I assure you, Mrs. Strawspinner, Frederick is so terribly ancient and so diminished in power I wasn't really sure he could do the stone-turning trick any more. I never thought he'd ever make such old bones—he's the leftover runt of a litter I had to make decades ago, and just kept him around for sentiment. He probably spent his last energy on Bogardus and it wouldn't surprise me if he didn't live till summer. Leave him be, hmmm? I'll be responsible. . . . We're old friends in a way, you see.

"And speaking of old friends," Delver continued, turning to King Oliver who was fanning himself with his crown, "I'd be obliged to have my gold returned. Like Frederick, don't really need it, but it's been around a long time and is as much part of me as anything else."

"Of course, of course." King Oliver snapped his fingers at the guards. Really, he thought, being King was getting to be quite interesting, even fun. "Take that statue back to the palace and put it in the gray dungeon for the time being—don't really want it standing around the palace; not what I'd call exactly a decorative or inspiring pose."

"Dungeon's as good a place as any, Your Majesty. Actually, I meant what I said. Frederick's powers *aren't* what they used to be and you may find in twenty or thirty years Bogardus coming back to life, hard to tell. Now I really must . . ." Delver seized the bellows again, intent on his alchemy.

Promising to send a brace of carpenters to repair the damage to Delver's cellar, King Oliver accepted Mrs. Strawspinner's invitation to midmorning coffee, which turned out to be not only coffee but a nut-and-apricot cake stuffed with whipped cream. Oliver, whimpering with delight, settled himself in the little bakery kitchen and went to work on it with a will.

Down below in the cellar, Andrew finished covering up Frederick's brazen vessel. The spaces under the archways didn't seem quite so forbidding now, but he was still glad he'd been unconscious when the Basilisk followed them into the tunnel. He only wished Sassie had been too.

"All done, sir." He handed the little shovel to Delver, who hung it carefully on the fireplace wall among all his other pokers, tongs, and tools.

"Splendid—splendid. Must get right to work now; never had such a rest in my life as those days in the dungeon. Feel full of fizzle, although I do say there's a lot of havoc to be repaired. Pity, but there you are. Not a bad job you did, by the way, although you put the Electrum back in the Orpiment phial and vice versa. However."

"Sir, could I ask two questions before we begin again?" Andrew took off his pointed hat, but held it in front of him, hoping it would remind Mr. Delver, who was champing at the bit waiting to get to work, of his responsibility to teach his Apprentice as well as use him.

"Drat it all. Well, proceed!"

"First of all, sir, what *is* the great Third Step? You've made a Philosopher's Stone, and you've made gold by using it; what else is there left to do?" Delver's eyebrows beetled furiously and Andrew rushed on. "If I *knew*, it'd help keep me *Eager*, sir!"

"Eager is one thing, being a quidnunc is another. However. You're right. The Third Step—oh, the beauty, the glory, when I attain it! I shall have a new robe, white I think— The Third Step is the Elixir of Life, Andrew, the Universal Panacea, cure for all ills! What could be more glorious—no sickness, nor malady, life forever— You see now my haste; it's a formidable task."

"Wow! Now I understand why the gold you

made doesn't seem very important compared to an Elixir of Life. Gee, Mr. Delver, when do we begin and how long will it take?"

"We begin now, of course, and it will take years, years, long after your Apprenticeship has expired and you've gone on to other things. I'll send you a postcard; let you know. Now. Second question?"

"Oh, well, after that maybe it doesn't seem very important. But the ham is all finished—I did make it last as long as I could, but it's gone, and so is the cheese, and—"

"You're wondering what you'll live on from now on? That's what I thought when I first set eyes on you—boys do have to eat, all the time. Well, perhaps a bit of barter with Mrs. Strawspinner—an hour or so of your time giving her a hand in exchange for a meal or two? Most economical for me, actually. Much of what needs to be done down here only I can do for some time to come, so your time is the cheapest commodity I have." Huzzah, Andrew thought, just what I hoped for! He started for the stairs, but Delver held up his hand impatiently.

"Before you go waltzing up there to stuff yourself, young man, you can set up the athanor and get the fire going—hazelwood fuel this time, if you please. Saturn ascends! And so do I; have a short errand. Keep up the work, lad." And Delver hitched his old puce robe around him and puffed up the stairs and out the green door.

"Sublime, utterly sublime. Mrs. Strawspinner, could I offer you the post of Supreme Chef of the palace kitchens? Never get anything decent to eat out of that vast barrackful of scullions and sous-chefs and sauciers and spit boys—might as well be cooked for by a plowman, the way it is now." King Oliver was more than halfway through the coffee cake and his third cup of coffee.

"Well, Your Majesty, you can offer but I won't accept. I like my own little business here just as it is. But I'll tell you what I'll do; saw the state of things long ago in your kitchen when I began making deliveries. First thing, you're understaffed, mostly numskulls too; your ovens are a scandal, your stove needs retiling, and it all smacks of Bogardus pinching your pennies so hard they slipped right into his own purse. Now there are one or two likely lads down there, and a scullery maid who's most promising indeed. I'll reorganize and train 'em and I'd say in two months you'll be eating better'n you have ever. And of course I'll continue my sweets and savories deliveries for you."

The tinkle of the little bell on the shop's door was followed by Sassie, who came into the kitchen leading Mr. Delver in an aura of cold air and a snowflake or two on his beard.

"Ah, Delver, just in time to share my small snack—you too, Miss Sassie. Sit you down, both of you, come along now. We've all had quite a morning!" Delver hemmed and hawed, standing on one foot, clearly eager to be gone. "No, Delver, I insist." King Oliver was growing more kingly and commanding every minute; Delver gingerly sat down and glared at the food on the table.

"We'll have to reorganize our schedule of horoscope and astronomy lessons, Delver. Now that I'm King on my own, I'll have a bit more responsibility, but we'll find the time, we'll find the time, don't worry about that. Fascinating subject . . ."

Andrew finished sweeping the floor around the athanor of the last chips of hazelwood, and watched the fire within the furnace settle into a very satisfactory slow burn. He neatly hung up the broom beside it, and looked about. Delver wasn't back from his errand yet, and he hadn't assigned any more tasks for the moment. It had been a long day and night; the state of Andrew's stomach was helping him to understand how desperate old Frederick must have been to have plowed through the tunnel for just a bit of bread and cheese. Lucky he was an old Basilisk and didn't eat much. Or he might have eaten Andrew and Sassie.

Eating. Hoping Delver's errand would keep him out long enough for Andrew to nip up and have a bite in the kitchen, he ran up the stairs and into the shop.

"Athanor stoked and going?" Great heavens, there was Delver himself actually sitting at Mrs. Strawspinner's table! On a chair! With the King! And Mrs. Strawspinner and Sassie too!

"Yessir!"

"Very well. Your pardon, Sire, but I have tasks below that cannot wait. You may have a quarter of an hour for breakfast, Andrew." Delver pushed back his chair and scurried out, with one disdainful glance at the mug of cocoa Mrs. Strawspinner was pouring out for Andrew.

"Maam, what's this package?" Sassie was holding a parcel wrapped in brown paper that had been on the floor by Delver's chair. "Oh, Mr. Delver must have left it. . . . Wait a minute; it has your name written on it, Andrew, backwards of course." She handed it to Andrew, who began unwrapping it.

"My bell! Sassie, it's my hand bell that was in the pawnshop!"

"Pawnshop? What's this about a pawnshop?" Sassie turned to the King and began explaining about Andrew, and his father, and his having to pawn the bell when he first arrived in the town, while Andrew sat, damp eyed, rubbing the brass of the bell lovingly with the old velvet of his jacket sleeve.

"Well, now, that's right nice, Andrew, of Mr. Delver to part with hard cash for your bell. He should be grateful, though; without you and Sassie he'd still be locked up in that dreadful cell. Now drink up your cocoa, lad, and have the last piece of nutcake— Land sakes, who ate that last piece?"

She looked fiercely around the table; the King shook his head ruefully as if he wished he had eaten it, and Sassie hadn't, and Andrew had clearly been looking forward to it when he came in. They all agreed there had been one small succulent piece left on the plate.

Suddenly Mrs. Strawspinner began to laugh. "I do believe . . . oh, Lordy, thought it'd never happen. . . . I really do believe Mr. Delver himself took it when he left! Never thought I'd live to see the day! Delver eating something! Well, no matter." And she opened one of her small oven doors, letting out an excruciating aroma of warm poppy seed, walnuts, and buttery sugar glaze. She slid the cake onto a plate and set it in front of Andrew.

"Try that on for size, young man, and give the King a piece while you're at it. Sassie and me too, come to think of it. But you'll have to make up your own mind whether or not you want to take a piece down cellar to Delver."

They all laughed, and Andrew said as he divided up the fresh pieces, "Golly, I don't know. Maybe Mr. Delver's like Frederick and only eats twice a year!"

BARBARA NINDE BYFIELD grew up in the West and Midwest, but has made her home in New York City for the last twenty years. She lives in an ancient farmhouse with seven fireplaces in Greenwich Village and has travelled extensively from Iceland to North Africa. She is the author-illustrator of *The Haunted Tower*, *The Book of Weird*, and other books for children, and has also written a number of mysteries for adults.

F   Byfield, Barbara
BYF   Ninde

        Andrew and the
        alchemist

DATE			
3D 4/3			
OCT 30			
DEC 19			
Feb 4			
APR. 28 1981			